What the Critics are saying:

A Perfect 10! "A hilarious romp...an irreverent cross between Janet Evanovich's Stephanie Plum and Laurell K. Hamilton's badass Anita Blake..." *~Kathy Samuels, Romance Reviews Today*

"This is a brilliantly written story...the heroine Desy is laugh-out-loud funny and Ms. Meadows has a fresh and humorous writing voice..." *~Angela Black, Sensual Romance*

"Fast action and off-beat humor characterize this first-in-a-series novel...the characters, situations and world-building are nothing less than spectacular..." *~Ann Leveille, Sensual Romance*

"...a highly entertaining paranormal story that exudes humor and sexuality..." *~Jennifer Wardrip, Romantic Times*

"...you won't be able to put it down...full of action and adventure, Something Wicked is a great read..." *~Angel Brewer, The Romance Studio*

"The heroine's dry sense of humor and occasional self-deprecating observations are simply hilarious...fast-paced, fun..." *~Mireya Orsini, Just Erotic Romance Reviews*

SOMETHING WICKED

By Jacqueline Meadows

Something Wicked
An Ellora's Cave Publication, August 2004

Ellora's Cave Publishing, Inc.
1337 Commerce Drive, Suite 13
Stow OH 44224

ISBN #1-8436-0906-1

Something Wicked © 2003 Jacqueline Meadows
ISBN MS Reader (LIT) ISBN # 1-84360-699-2
Other available formats (no ISBNs are assigned):
Adobe (PDF), Rocketbook (RB), Mobipocket (PRC) & HTML

Edited by: *Raelene Gorlinsky*
Cover art by: *Syneca*

Warning:

The following material contains graphic sexual content meant for mature readers. *Something Wicked* has been rated *E-rotic* by a minimum of three independent reviewers.

Ellora's Cave Publishing offers three levels of Romantica™ reading entertainment: S (S-ensuous), E (E-rotic), and X (X-treme).

S-*ensuous* love scenes are explicit and leave nothing to the imagination.

E-*rotic* love scenes are explicit, leave nothing to the imagination, and are high in volume per the overall word count. In addition, some E-rated titles might contain fantasy material that some readers find objectionable, such as bondage, submission, same sex encounters, forced seductions, etc. E-rated titles are the most graphic titles we carry; it is common, for instance, for an author to use words such as "fucking", "cock", "pussy", etc., within their work of literature.

X-*treme* titles differ from E-rated titles only in plot premise and storyline execution. Unlike E-rated titles, stories designated with the letter X tend to contain controversial subject matter not for the faint of heart.

Chapter 1

Just one short week ago I was your average, run-of-the-mill girl, normal in every way. My only concerns were cottage cheese thighs, world peace, my aunt's health, or what to wear on my next date. See, common things. Ordinary.

Not so anymore. Nope. In the span of a few short days my entire world has been turned upside down. Now I have men trouble, two to be exact. Virile, sinfully handsome and accomplished, both fine specimens, each vying for me. Catch the virile and sinfully handsome part? You see the problem—it's an impossible choice.

My picture's been spread all over the papers, too. That was a nasty surprise, believe you me. My job's mostly undercover, I work as a private investigator, a gumshoe, and private detectives need to remain, well, private. Being splashed all over the newspaper is not a good thing.

But the real biggy? Turns out I'm some kind of High Priestess, a Wiccan Queen of all things pagan and mystical. Ha! Little ol' me, go figure. Except I don't *exactly* know how to control my supernatural powers yet. There've been some…problems.

And oh yeah, I think I killed a man. Sort of. The details are still a bit fuzzy.

I know. I know. Sounds like I had a few too many during happy hour, doesn't it? But cross my heart, it's the truth.

How'd this all come about? Glad you asked.

It all started when *he* came to town and well, it just sort of snowballed from there. It was last Monday. I remember it distinctly because we were well into spring, three full weeks of pleasant warmth, sunshine, birds chirping merrily, and then it snowed. Welcome to Michigan.

That morning I'd planned on wearing a nice cotton sundress with a matching jacket. The outfit has a small floral pattern, cute but not cutesy, paired with spanking new sandals, neutral, two-inch heels. (Believe me, when you're as vertically challenged as I am, you need the extra help.)

But it was all a no-go because Mother Nature was having a bad day. So instead, I dug out a lightweight turtleneck in a soft mocha brown, pulled on a matching skirt and boots, slapped on some makeup, a coat, and I was good to go. Out the door in twenty minutes flat.

I drove to work at warp speed over patched and bumpy roads in my trusty black Jeep. The odometer reads over eighty thousand, it has a temperamental stereo, an annoying squeak in the rear seat, and an exterior that has seen better days, but I can always count on it starting.

The same sense of eager anticipation coursed through me that morning I feel every day for my job because although a paycheck is nice, great in fact, work means much more than that to me. My name's on the sign out front, Sage and Phatt Investigations. I'm Phatt. No snickering, you can imagine all the fat jokes I've been the brunt of over the years, so don't start. I've heard 'em all; you'd only be repeating.

And Sage? He's my partner, Nicholas Sage. I call him Nick for short or, if I really want to irritate him, Nicky. My Nick is a gorgeous guy, six-foot-one, ex-quarterback, blond hair, blue eyes, all-American. You get the picture. If you look at him long enough, I guarantee drool will start to trickle down your chin. I've seen it happen time and time again, but he's strictly off-limits, at least that's what I tell myself each and every day. The problem? There's a shiny gold ring on his left hand. My Nick's married.

Notice I didn't say happily married. That's because he's not. See, Anita, his wife? Well, they were dating when she told him she was pregnant and being the great guy he is, he immediately did the right thing and married her. Then lo and behold after the deed was done and sacred vows exchanged, she waits two-three months and says Oops, there's no baby—she made a mistake, by golly. Premeditated? Entrapment? You tell me.

He's trying to make the best of it, though, and obviously there's something there or long ago he'd have called Divorces 'R' Us. It's been a couple years now. Talk remains sparse about Anita and their relationship, and I don't pry, but you can tell he's been forced to make lemonade out of a whopper of a lemon. I hoped the taste wasn't proving too sour.

I've known Nick all my life. His family owned the house right next to mine and we grew up together. Best friends for years. I watched him graduate from training wheels to two-wheeler, heard his voice break from high soprano to a deep, smooth bass, watched him fill out and transform from middle school acne geek to high school football quarterback and prom king. I saw girls swoon around him in college and promised myself I wouldn't be one of them. Ever. No way. Not me.

We're just friends. Completely platonic. Am I protesting too much?

Anyway, his father started the detective business and Nick just naturally fell into it. And because Nick did, so did I. His father's retired now, lives with the little missus down in Florida where I'm sure it doesn't snow in May. A couple years ago we added my name to the sign.

Don't get me wrong, it wasn't a free ride for me, I put in my time—lots of grunt work throughout high school for his dad and four years of college studying the investigative field, law enforcement, even a few credits of criminal justice. I earned my PI license. I'm a full partner. I know what I'm doing. Most of the time.

* * * * *

When I pulled into the thin alley behind our building that morning, Nick's red 'vette was already there, parked on an obscene angle—ostensibly to avoid dings—and I remember thinking 'Damn' because it meant suffering through his coffee—bitter, thick sludge. Ick. Yuck. Gag. Rule is first one in makes the coffee.

Snow, now this, I mourned. I didn't know then that as the day and week wore on, it would just get worse. A lot worse.

I hopped from my Jeep, trudged through three inches of spring snow. A little bell merrily tinkled hello when I pushed open the back door. Voices traveled down the hall as I stomped my wet boots and hung up my coat, wondering if we were already up and running that early. See, clients park out front, but since I arrive at work from the rear, I usually only see the building's butt-ugly backend.

A brisk stride took me around the corner to find Nick handing a 40-ish woman a tissue. She sat quietly weeping. His uncomfortable, near-frantic gaze found mine over her blond head and I literally saw relief fill his baby blues. Nick never knows what to do with weepy women.

"Mrs. Lowell?" he said. "Here's my associate, Ms. Phatt." I shook her limp hand. She continued to sniffle and Nick told her, "I'll just get you a cup of coffee. Why don't you tell Ms. Phatt a little more about your situation?"

He hightailed it across the room and began the ritual of pouring our potential client coffee...in slow motion. He's an expert at tactical avoidance, especially when estrogen runs high.

Mrs. Lowell was a pale blond, attractive, slim, dressed well and expensively in a linen pantsuit of light green under a black wool, three-quarter-length coat. Ankle boots, Prada; I tried not to salivate overmuch. Jewelry flashed from her ears, neck and hands.

"It's a pleasure to meet you, Mrs. Lowell," I said, grabbing the laptop from Nick's desk. "Would you like a few minutes? May I take your coat?" She shook her head and blinked red-rimmed eyes of sad hazel. "All right," I said, sitting. "How may we be of help to you?"

"I think my husband's having an affair."

I schooled my features to remain pleasant but noncommittal and mentally sighed, remembering the first few times I'd heard that line. Shocking and sad then, but now, after dozens of similar cases, I closed in on numb. Almost there. I'd certainly lost my naiveté and the belief in happily-ever-after. Call me a cynic, but when you've seen what I've seen, you can no longer dance carefree at weddings. The odds aren't all that great the happy couple's union will outlast the warranty on their new four-slice toaster.

"I'm sorry, Mrs. Lowell. What has aroused your suspicion?"

She tucked the used tissue in her purse. "Frank has been working quite late recently. When I call his office, though, they say he's either not there or unable to answer the phone." She cleared her throat. "And then there's this." From her purse Mrs. Lowell pulled a small scrap of paper, the edges jagged as if carelessly torn from a larger piece. "It was in his pants pocket," she added softly.

I took the scrap from her. A phone number for *Michelle* looped across its face, written in wavy, curly handwriting. Pink ink. A small heart floated above the 'i'. How cute.

Nick returned with two coffees, passed one to Mrs. Lowell and parked mine on the low table near my knee. As he rejoined the conversation, questioning her further, I tapped away at the laptop entering pertinent information. With said husband's picture, schedule, and place of work on record, we settled on our fee; she chose to pay in cash—a down payment that morning and the balance when the job was complete.

As Nick wrote a receipt, Mrs. Lowell took a sip of coffee. And grimaced. I met her horror-filled gaze in silent commiseration, watched as she placed the wicked brew on the table and gingerly nudged it away. By lunch, that one swallow would probably eat a hole in her stomach lining. I suspect my own resembles Swiss cheese by now.

We thanked her, walked her to the door. Nick told her to expect our call soon.

He turned to me after she left and drawled, "Morning, Desy." That's me, short for Desdemona. "I'm still tangled up with paperwork on the Whitcomb case," he said. "Can you start on this one?"

I said, "Sure thing," and turned to my desk. We have one large open room instead of separate offices. His dad set it up like this. "I'll need your laptop for a sec."

"No problem." He reached for it and spied my untouched coffee on the table. It sat there looking lonely and innocent, but I knew better. "And your coffee too?" he asked.

"No." I mock shuddered. "That cup can stay there and grow mold...or hair, whichever happens first. You see," I mused, "I think I may want to have children someday...and it's pure conjecture at this point, but I believe your coffee causes irreparable internal damage. Maybe even complete sterility."

A noise rumbled in his throat, the sound halfway between chuckle and snort, before he handed me the laptop.

Chapter 2

Stakeouts are every bit as boring as you imagine them to be. I've always assumed most cop vigils were slightly better than mine because they at least worked in pairs and got to eat doughnuts.

I have to watch my figure. Be ever vigilant. At five foot two and one centimeter, the closest I've ever come to ingesting doughnuts is breathing the yeast-scented air as I drive past the corner bakery. Greedy, I whiz by and often gulp two, three mouthfuls. No one's the wiser.

No, stakeouts were the pits, until I discovered books on tape. Now I can feel my ass fall asleep as I listen to the dulcet tones of an author reading to me. Who could ask for more?

The sky cleared as I sat parked for over two hours in front of Mr. Lowell's place of business, the snow having long since stopped. Three cheers for spring—hip hip hooray.

He finally exited the building at six-fifteen and I must admit, the photograph didn't do him justice. No, our Mr. Lowell was quite a well-kept masculine specimen, mid-forties, fit. I couldn't make out his physique too well under the unbuttoned full-length coat but he was a spiffy dresser, handsome, black hair with just a touch of gray at the sides. Distinguished.

He left the parking lot in a dark tan Mercedes-Benz SL320 convertible. I knew he worked in computer technology of some sort. Obviously, Frank did quite well for himself, I thought.

I logged the time and followed along two car lengths behind him.

Earlier that day I'd plugged mysterious Michelle's phone number into my computer, unearthed a recent class picture of her over the 'net. Handy tool, that. Turned out she was a college student majoring in art over at the local university who still lived at home with mommy. I know—I called. Acted like an old high school pal trying to track her down and the ruse worked so well, mom and I became quite chummy. We talked for a bit and I'm sure I could have discovered Michelle's bra size if I'd wanted to. What I did discover was that she had a date that night: Michelle Burne, all of 19 years old, and possibly doing the dirty deed with married Mr. Lowell, age 46.

Speaking of Mr. Lowell, he merged onto the I-75 freeway north and passed the exit that would have taken him safely home into the waiting arms of his loving wife.

It looked like I was in business, and none too soon. My book tape just concluded. The main characters fell in love and a happy ending was had by all. Yippee. Fiction's great.

He exited at Big Beaver Road (the sexual connotations of which make me snicker each time I pass the street) and turned left toward the row of upscale hotels. The Mercedes's blinker flashed right and he turned into the Marclay Inn. Bingo.

I cruised by as he pulled into a parking spot third row from the front entrance and had just scrambled from my Jeep when he entered through the large glass doors.

If he played slap-and-tickle that evening, the best I could hope for in a hotel like the Marclay was some obvious canoodling in open areas—say the lobby, elevator, hallway, parking lot. You can't very well catch someone in the act five floors up with the blinds and door closed. Houdini I'm not.

I followed him straight through the lobby past large potted plants and cozy sectional seating to the hotel bar. He paused to scan the dimly lit room before sliding onto a stool, and ordered a scotch on the rocks as I walked by. Soft rock played in the background, the lead singer agonizing in mournful tones over his lost love.

I chose my seat quickly but with care. And waited. That's the thing about my profession, the waiting. There's lots of it. You have to be patient and luckily, I am. So's Nick.

Know how private eyes are always portrayed on television? Bang, bang and cuff 'em Charlie? Fictional. Wrong. You can't go round shooting at suspects or even call up your friendly cop on vice and ask him to peek at some records for you. That's all illegal. PI's don't have any more rights than regular citizens do. Now if I ruled the universe? They would. Absolutely.

A test has to be passed, a special license applied for, just to be armed; and I better only shoot at someone in self-defense, be able to prove it, or I'll wind up next to Big Bertha in a ten by seven. Not a pretty thought.

Anyway, there I sat on my second sparkling water with lemon, when in waltzed a tall young brunette and without the slightest pause, crossed straight to the bar to perch on the stool beside married Mr. Lowell.

I whipped out my cell phone as Michelle leaned into him and planted a long, hot one right on his 46-year-old mouth. Wondering about my cell phone? Well, it really isn't, it's a spy camera. Neato, huh? It looks just like the real thing but all the time I appear as if I'm blabbing away to a friend, in actuality I'm snapping pictures, and I got some doozies of the happy couple. My camera has 10x zoom, infrared, digital, all the bells and whistles. I managed to get some good close-ups — tongues, spit and all.

Quicker than a New York minute, they left the bar and after making a hasty pit stop at the front desk, hurried hand-in-hand to the elevators.

I overheard their room number, 326. A separate elevator shuttled me to the third floor and I managed to snap some more shots before they fell into their room, tangled limbs, locked lips, laughing.

Poor Mrs. Lowell.

Back to waiting. I decided to do mine in luxury down in the lobby. It was ten past seven — who knew how long Mr. Lowell could last?

I made my way toward the bank of sectionals near the fake roaring fire and silk palm trees, and a commotion to my left caught my eye. The celebrated mayor of nearby Detroit City and his lovely wife walked toward me, a half dozen noisy reporters in tow. The group headed for the elevators.

And that's when a thief or, as I refer to him, an idiot with obvious shit for brains, decided to snatch Mrs. Mayor's three-hundred-dollar Coach purse. His intellect obviously rivaled that of a garden tool's. I mean, didn't he recognize the mayor? See the reporters? Evidently not. The purse snagged on her shoulder and he actually knocked her down.

Lights flashed.

I was on him before you could say tae-kwon-do. Hadn't planned it or given it a second thought, just ran up the couch, jumped off its back, and flew through the air with the greatest of ease to land solidly on the guy. Tackled him flat.

All around me flashes of light popped.

Now, I weigh only about a hundred pounds soaking wet so this beefy brainiac tried bucking me off, then cursing me off, and when neither worked, he squirmed and managed to land a punch. His fist glanced off my mouth, busted my lip. I tasted blood.

That got my dander up, but good.

I twisted his arm back and bent one of his fingers until he squealed like a little piggy with no roast beef.

Snapping here and there, more lights flashed.

Help came then in the form of hotel security: two burly guards. I sat squarely on his back as they cuffed him. Then I stood, straightened my hair and clothes, found Mrs. Mayor's purse, and walked to her (a little unsteadily I admit). I silently handed it over.

That's when it dawned on me what all the flashes of light were about. Cameras. Reporters. Shit. They swarmed all around me like killer bees from a downed hive. Buzzing. Questioning. Shouting.

I kept repeating, "No comment" and pushed my way through the inquisitive horde, past the lobby's glass doors to fresh air, and kept right on going until I reached my Jeep.

I drove home that night while room 326 steamed up, a married woman sat home alone once again, no doubt crying, and with my lip throbbing in time to the latest Red Hot Chili Peppers CD.

I played it so loud my Jeep vibrated.

Chapter 3

Around eight that night I pulled into my driveway.

I live with my Aunt Penelope. Both my parents died in a car accident when I was just a baby. Aunt P raised me. She's the only parent I've ever known and I couldn't love her more.

That's why I'm still here with her in this big ol' Victorian and not out on my own. She's getting on in years now, nearing seventy-five, and although she can still run circles around me on one of her good days, I just feel the need to look after her, be nearby.

Our house is plop in the center of middle-class suburbia, complete with tree-lined streets, kids playing on sidewalks, and nice green lawns. In summer, the ice cream truck drives by daily, chirping its familiar happy song through open windows and rooftop speakers. We're wedged between the urban decay of Detroit and the filthy rich of the northern 'burbs; if you have to be wedged, it's not a bad place to be—sort of like living between the Haves and the Have-Nots in the vast land of the Have-Somes.

My street is nestled in a small enclave of historic homes, overflowing with English Tudors, angles, peaks, and endless upkeep. Aunt P is quite, well, I'll say *adventurous* with color. (Do I get brownie points for being polite?) Our front door is painted a shocking chartreuse and the house trim varies from shades of dusty purple to bold wine red. You either love the house or loathe it. Won't tell you which side I fall on.

From the foyer I called, "Aunt P? I'm home!" and her answer echoed, "In the sunroom." After stuffing my winter coat in the closet, I made my way there.

Huge purple flowers scream from the material covering the sunroom's couch, and Aunt P sat among the garish posies and large matching pillows—but she didn't sit alone. No, next to her sat my private fantasy come to life of the perfect male. Longish dark hair, right on the cusp of black, sculpted face and body, not too tall—maybe around five foot eleven or thereabouts. Looked like he wore a suit costing more than I pull down in a good month; Armani, I believe.

And he stared at me as if he were a castaway and I was a nice, fat goose that miraculously wandered onto his sandy island. Dark, hungry eyes never veered as he stood.

"Desy, I'd like you to meet Armand Bellamy," my aunt said. "His father and I were old, dear friends. He passed away last year. Armand's been kind enough to visit from Paris." She beamed. "This is Desdemona."

As my stomach performed a circus trick, a slow spinning somersault, then two, I found my vocal cords. "Hi, Mr. Bellamy. It's a pleasure to meet you." My voice emerged quite normal, not vapid or breathy, and I silently congratulated myself.

We shook hands.

"Please, call me Armand, and the pleasure is mine." He brought my hand to his mouth, pressed a soft kiss on my knuckles. Yowza. I'd only seen that done in old black and white movies. It was even better in living color.

His voice poured rich like smooth dark honey, accented with French...and sex. Charming, mannered, gorgeous—all in one handy, stunning package. Flustered, I took back my hand and my ire roused as his lips curved in a slight, knowing smile.

"Let's move to the kitchen," Aunt P invited. "Have you had dinner yet, Desy?"

I shook my head no, trying not to stare at him.

"Good. Armand has made us a fabulous meal." Of course he had. Why was I not surprised? He'd probably vacuumed, cleaned the windows, and fixed the leaky faucet upstairs before assembling cucumber sandwiches and petit fours. "What is it called again, dear?" Aunt P asked him.

Armand motioned for us to proceed him into the kitchen. "It's *Bordeau Chesnel*, a simple pot roast, I'm afraid."

Modest too.

I had a few questions for Mr. Bellamy but I held my tongue throughout the meal; besides, it was too busy sampling his roast to be of much help.

✶ ✶ ✶ ✶ ✶

"How did you come by your injury?" he asked.

"Injury?"

He leaned toward me and brushed his thumb in a soft caress, feather-light, over my busted lip. I stilled, pulled my face away, and he settled in his chair wearing that same knowing smile I first experienced in the sunroom. It curved faint and self-satisfied. Cocky. I didn't like it.

My hand rose automatically to my bottom lip and fingered the split, still swollen and lightly throbbing. The salt from dinner had aggravated it, but the sharp sting felt worthy of the wonderful meal. The man could cook. Living on Lean Cuisines, I'd forgotten what real food tasted like.

"Oh, it's nothing," I said, skirting his question.

He raised an eyebrow at my evasion.

We were alone, sitting across from each other in the living room. Two lamps softly illuminated the couches, chairs, wall hangings (mostly botanical prints — my aunt's favorite), and the odd assortment of occasional tables.

Aunt P went to bed right after dinner. Conveniently. In her wake I smelled the subtle scent of matchmaking, cloying and unwelcome.

"So, Mr. Bellamy —"

"Armand, please."

"Armand. Um, I didn't see your car out front." I waited a beat but he didn't respond. "Do you need a ride somewhere tonight? A hotel perhaps?"

He smiled and his teeth flashed white. "No, but thank you for your kind concern." His expression told me he knew neither kindness *nor* concern fueled my question. "Your aunt has graciously invited me to stay here," he explained, "with you."

Wonderful. He crossed his legs and his black shoes, polished to a high sheen, winked at me. The posture didn't look the least bit effeminate, but rather oddly graceful. "I believe she placed me in the room opposite yours."

Double wonderful. My heart deflated and sank, like a child's lost balloon. "Hmm. How long will you be staying with us?" My question knowingly skimmed right along the border between slight prying and flat-out rude.

"That depends on you." His voice, thick and rich, poured over me like expensive French chocolate. Not that I've eaten expensive chocolate before, French or otherwise. Usually just a few M&M's do the trick. Still, his voice...I wanted to wallow in it and at that disturbing thought, my lips pursed and I chewed briefly on the inside of my mouth, a nasty habit.

"How so?" I asked.

"I need time alone with you. We have much to discuss, you and I."

My forehead scrunched at his puzzling words. Time alone? Much to discuss? Hindsight being 20-20, this is where I should have just shown him the door. Right that very minute. But I didn't know what was to come. How could I?

He continued, "It's too late tonight to begin. Are you free tomorrow? Perhaps we could spend some time together?"

I scratched my head, remembered to blink. "I work...and tomorrow's Tuesday. I've got an Aikijutsu class at six and then a date."

I started attending martial arts classes at the age of ten and a few bruised years later, earned a black belt in karate. Needing a new challenge, I took up Aikijutsu about three months ago. Took up with the instructor shortly after that. His name's Chen Kincaid and he owns and operates three martial arts facilities. After two months of dinners, movies and plays, Tuesday was to be my first gander at his downtown loft. I was comfortable with Chen and liked him enough to dive forward to second base, perhaps even third. He's a nice guy. Sweet.

"Wednesday, then?" Armand asked, persistent.

I shifted in the chair. "What do you need to talk to me about?"

"Is Wednesday open, Desdemona?"

I frowned slightly at his doggedness. "Call me Desy and yes, I suppose Wednesday is okay if a hot case doesn't pop up by then."

"Good. Wednesday it is. Would you share an early dinner with me that evening?"

I cocked my head and considered him. I didn't like how I felt around him, like if he crooked his finger, I just might lunge. He was entirely too good-looking, a complete stranger. It somehow raised my hackles, and my intuition screamed — why or what, I didn't know, but it definitely warned me about something. I ignored it. Stupid, right?

"Sure. Around five sound okay?"

"*Oui*, yes."

"All right." I stood and he followed me up. "I don't know about you, but I'm bushed. Do you need anything before I go to bed?"

"*Non*, but thank you." He clasped my hand, kissed its back. "*Passer une bonne nuit*," he murmured against my skin. "*Faites de beau reves*."

I shivered and took back my hand, rubbed it. "What does that mean?"

His dark, intense gaze searched my face; I watched it land on every feature before his eyes returned to mine and locked on.

"Have a good night's sleep." With a slow smile he added, "Sweet dreams."

I murmured, "You too," after a long hard swallow, and I floated up the stairs.

* * * * *

That night I dreamt.

My slumbering reverie was striking in form, amusing at times, and all-too-fleeting; nevertheless, it is a tiny jewel of a memory, one that I carry around in a small pocket of my mind and when the mood strikes, pull it out for viewing.

The dream had a chalky, hazy quality as I padded down the darkened hall from my bedroom to his, bare feet soundless on the cold hardwood floor. The quiet tick of antique clocks was the only noise in the sleeping house. Armand's door swung open before I turned its knob and one large hand pulled me inside. He backed me up against the closed door, body flush with mine, a thick erection sandwiched between our bellies, and in a velvet voice, as dark and warm as the room, he murmured, "It's about time, *mon chou.*"

"What?"

He eased my robe off and as it puddled at my ankles, my heart pounded almost painfully. "What took you so long?" Armand chastised. "Half the night is gone." He cupped my breasts. The size and warmth of his hands wrenched a soft sound from my throat as he rolled my nipples in a hot, tugging pinch between forefinger and thumb, shooting fiery prickles straight to my womb.

I gasped, clutched at his biceps, nails digging into his flesh while shock and arousal hammered through me. "Wait…wait a goddamn minute here…this is a dream. My dream! You're not supposed to say that!"

A smooth chuckle brushed against my cheek and he squeezed my breasts in a burning crush, molding them beneath his broad hands. "*Excusez-moi, mademoiselle*, I'm unaware of a script. What should I say instead?" Along my lips, his tongue traced a wet path, sensuous and molten, ardent, and from deep within my throat, a small traitorous moan slipped free.

"God, I don't know," I breathed. "Something soft and sweet would be nice."

He caught the lobe of my right ear between his teeth and nibbled before whispering, "Marshmallow."

Under the wet roar of his tongue burrowing inside my ear and two caressing hands squeezing, plumping my breasts as thoroughly as a sculptor molding clay, my mind turned the word over. I couldn't have heard him right. "Wh…What did you say?!"

His tongue left my ear. "Marshmallow—something soft and sweet." My startled laugh mixed with Armand's long pleasure-filled hum as his hands left my breasts, blazed down my spine, and filled with my ass. He squeezed. The motion again plastered his cock, hot and straining, against me, sending my entire body into one long, giddy shudder. "Where do you want it?" he whispered. "Bed? Wall? Chair? All three perhaps? After all, this *is* your dream."

I snorted. "My dream? *Marshmallow* is whispered to me as a sweet nothing, there's not a shred of romance, and it's so dark in here even an owl couldn't see! This is so *not* my dream!"

Armand's hands stroked the backs of my thighs. "It's dark our first time because you've made it so, and soft romance, whispered sweet nothings, are far from what you want tonight."

"They are?"

He lifted me, hands curved around my thighs, spreading me wide. "*Oui.* What you want is this." There was no hesitation, no fumbling. He plunged inside me in one long thrust.

"Jesus Christ!" I cried.

"*Non*, call me Armand."

My strangled laugh spiked into a sharp moan at the first pump of his hips. Broad and lengthy, his cock felt enormous, and I wound myself around him in an eager embrace, arms and legs wrapped tight, as he slid back and forth, rocking my back in a lazy tempo against the door. His body heat enveloped me, his slow rhythm enticed with leisurely thrusts, circling hips, while the mesmerizing feel of him—muscles, firm flesh, soft hair brushing my cheek, breath panting in my ear, his scent—branded me, made me throb and pulse and ache and want. I slipped under. Drowned.

"You are *magnifique*. Tight...and wet...and unbelievably...perfect." He licked my nipple in a fiery wash and sucked, drew it deep inside his mouth. In quick succession, my stomach performed three soaring backflips. Dizzy, I closed my eyes and felt my clitoris sing when he brushed it again on his next upstroke. My insides twisted, coiling with a hot pulse, and another moan spilled from my mouth.

His rhythm sped—cock pounding in thick, forceful digs, slick glides, wet noises, every long inch stretching me, until I tightened with the onrush of release.

Hot against my breast Armand whispered, "Now, *mon chou*." He pinched my nipple between his teeth, a stinging wet prick, and from head to toe my flesh tingled and flamed, shook in a clenching grip. I dashed higher and higher and higher. "Now," he breathed.

Armand filled me with wet heat, spraying thick jets of cream, and my sharp cry joined with his moan as I convulsed, spasming tight around his cock.

My eyes flew open. I woke with that cry filling my small bedroom, my bones melting into the sheets, and a rocketing orgasm just starting to recede. Panting, I turned my head to stare at the glowing hands of my bedside alarm clock—4:03 a.m.—and I knew only one thing: if I fell back to sleep quickly enough, I might be able to squeeze in another dream before my alarm rang.

Chapter 4

Squeaks sounded as I wiped steam from the bathroom mirror and gazed at my reflection. I frowned. Since day one my hair has had a mind of its own. I have baby pictures as proof. Doesn't matter what I want it to do, doesn't care about current cuts or fads, it just does its own one thing — curl — and lots of 'em. Corkscrews, long and bouncy, coil willy nilly all over my head.

Now I know some women actually pay good money for this 'do, but it's a little different when you have no choice. And the color? Brown. Neither light nor dark, just middle-of-the-road, plain dirt brown. Like my eyes.

And while critiquing, I have to admit I've always thought my mouth a little too wide, my lips a bit overfull, until collagen injections became all the rage. Now I can pucker with the best of them and think gleefully of all the money I'm saving.

But the thing you might notice first is my skin — it's swarming with freckles. My freckles literally have freckles. A game of connect-the-dots would take you days...weeks even. I can never quite achieve the femme fatale look with these little brown dots peppering me. It just doesn't work. I'm forever stuck akin with Rebecca of Sunny Brook Farm.

My only saving grace from resembling a grownup, dimpled Shirley Temple is my figure — it's curvy, and my chest is quite, well, let's say healthy.

I remember trying to pull a comb through my wet hair that morning and groaning at the bathroom clock. My lip felt stiff but no longer swollen as I brushed my pearly whites.

Finished, I capped the toothpaste, whipped open the bathroom door and smacked into warm, male flesh. A chest.

Firm muscles, soft fleece. Large hands grasped my shoulders and steadied me. I looked up. Armand.

"Sorry." I swallowed. "Um, it's all yours. I'm ah, done."

There's only one full bathroom upstairs. That's how they used to build houses in the good ol' days and until that morning, I never felt it a problem.

I stood nude and slightly damp under my terrycloth robe and he had donned only a pair of worn tight jeans, the top button undone. I know. I peeked.

Armand murmured *"Bonjour,"* and slowly leaned his head toward mine. The bathroom's steam swirled around us and the air grew thick and moist as he closed in. I gazed at his mouth a mere inch from my own, breathed, "What are you doing?" and watched it open, felt his warm breath feather over me as he whispered, "Kissing you."

And he did.

I didn't react at first. Maybe it was just the shock of my mouth spitting toothpaste down the drain one minute and pressing against warm, French lips the next. Call me slow, but I needed a few seconds to adjust.

He moved against my mouth in long, lazy brushes. Rubbing. Coaxing. It was apparent he had practice, and lots of it. I parted my lips and he sank inside, tongue swirling hot against mine, tasting of warm sleep and experience. I imagined mine tasted of Crest tartar control with whitening agents.

It was when he closed the inch between our bodies, brushing flush against me that I ended our game of tonsil hockey. An erection bulged high. A big one. That and the disconcerting fact that had he only asked, I'd have gladly exchanged more bodily fluids with him than just saliva. The thought was chilling. He was the son of my aunt's dearly departed friend, a complete stranger, and although he played a starring role in last night's nocturnal fantasy, things were moving a bit too fast in real life.

I edged away, opened my mouth to speak, closed it when my mind blanked. Opened it again and at the sight of his warm, slightly amused smile, snapped it shut and made a small, annoyed humph sound.

I turned and padded down the hall to my bedroom, licked my lips en route and tasted blood. Shit! I fumed—he'd reopened my cut.

* * * * *

Eight o'clock and I'd just finished pouring water into the trusty office's Bunn when in strolled Nick. Carrying a rolled-up newspaper under one arm and a box of fresh bagels one-handed, he beelined to me through the wafting sweet aroma of Folgers Classic Roast.

"Morning, handsome," I said.

He leaned against my desk (it's the closest to the coffeemaker—lucky me) and casually crossed one leg over the other. The thing about knowing someone for years is that although he looked calm that morning, he really wasn't. Nope. I could tell.

"And you're giving me the evil eye because…"

"Well," he began, "is there anything you'd like to tell me?"

I cocked my head and stared at him. The tone he used—part condescending, part hovering big brother—boiled my innards. "Sure, Nicky, I'm game," and I tapped a finger against my chinny-chin-chin. "Let's see…I'm wearing a new dress today. Got it at Needless Markups—uh, Neiman Marcus—50% off. Oh, my lingerie, too, all new, made of stretchy white lace, really quite comfy. I made an appointment next week for my six-month dental checkup. Broke a nail yesterday. I returned a video late and discovered the store jacked up their fees *again*—this time another whole buck. Absolute highway robbery. Got a date tonight with Chen at his place after class and I'm thinking of allowing some petting. You know, groping hands, body parts?

Nothing too heavy, though, it's just that he's waited patiently for weeks. What do you think?"

I folded my arms and waited. It didn't take long.

During my monologue his jaw firmed to a hard line and by the time I finished, a little tic started near his left eye, pulling slightly on his cheek—the sign for imminent danger. I smiled.

Nick sucked in a calming breath, set the bagels on my desk and unrolled the newspaper, flattening the middle crease. "I think it's too soon for Chip and you'd better take a look at this."

"Chen," I corrected and peered at the paper he held. My gaze started at the top headlines and traveled south, snagging on a picture that filled the entire bottom third of the front page. The headline read 'Unidentified Woman Stops Thief—Saves Mayor's Wife'. The picture showed me sitting squarely on shit-for-brain's back in the hotel lobby, viciously bending his arm and finger backwards. I was grinning.

I straightened, both hands flew to my mouth and under them I gasped, "Oh hell!"

Nick barked a humorless laugh and said, "It gets worse. More pictures are inside and the entire article is slanted to create a frenzy to discover your name." He dropped the paper on my desk. "The mayor and his wife want to take you to dinner to express their gratitude for your bravery. They're quoted as joking about offering a reward for your identity."

My arms fell dead and limp, useless at my sides. "Oh shit!"

"And the police, of course."

"The police?" I managed to squeak.

"They need your statement for their case. You'll probably have to testify at the trial as well."

Of course I would. What had I been thinking? "Damn!"

Nick pivoted, grabbed a fish bowl from behind the Bunn, and silently held it out. Fuming, I chewed the inside of my mouth. Dubbed the cussing bowl, each time one of us cursed we owed it one buck. Dollar bills—mostly mine—filled the bowl halfway.

I fished a dollar from my purse and tossed it in. Nick held up three wiggling fingers, flashing his devilish smile. He's good at that one. Got it down pat. I stuck out my tongue, the action juvenile but satisfying, and threw in two more bills.

Chapter 5

My opponent stood around six-foot-one with a weight more than double my own, looking in dire need of a good shave and some Eau De Smell-Better Cologne for men.

Chen paired us, whether from sick humor or complete confidence in my abilities, I didn't know. Either way, my twitching nerves didn't show. When the situation calls for one, I have a great poker face.

My gaze swept the sidelines for my guy and I smiled at his sly wink.

Chen's the progeny of an Asian mother and American father. Born and raised one hundred percent U.S.A. grade A beefcake, he's a real looker, as Aunt P would say, and did, when she met him last month. Blurted it out right to his face. Gotta love her, the older she gets, the sassier she turns. A real hoot.

Anyway, Chen stands around five-ten-ish or so, muscled but lean, patrician features bordering on pretty, with black silky hair fanning to his shoulders. I know his hair is silky because I've buried my hands in it frequently. Chen's a nice kisser.

The cymbals sounded and after sharing bows, my opponent charged me. New to the class, he committed a novice's error by taking one look at little me and deciding the bout already won. Finished. Done.

Wrong.

A defensive art, Aikijutsu is similar to karate. I like it because it's a unique mix of using leverage and striking at weak points, and because a pipsqueak like me can whup ass and take down names.

I waited until whisker-face stood just about on top of me, grabbed his forearms, and dropped backwards. As he followed me down, I jammed both feet into his gut and flipped him over my head. He landed on the mat with a great satisfying thud and wheeze. I sprang up and waited.

Rule is we had to go at it until one opponent signals to quit or the cymbals bong, whichever occurs first. I remember having the feeling I'd have to wait for the cymbals that match because when five-o'clock-shadow stood, he looked determined and royally ticked.

I crouched in a defensive stance and watched him barrel at me again. Man, he looked steamed as he charged—eyes spitting mad, just this side of wild, and cheeks flushed livid. It no longer felt like a practice session. When he was within range, I used a two-leg kick and admittedly, my strike was a little off. Okay, okay, a lot off. I've practiced since and improved, but that night I aimed for his solar plexus and while one foot did land there, well, the other lodged squarely against his gonads. I fell to the mat on my side, legs stinging, and after flying backwards, my opponent landed hard on his back, rolled immediately to his side and curled into a tight moaning ball.

The cymbals sounded, match over.

I bowed to the lump of masculine agony and crossed to the sidelines. Chen's face pulled into a slight grimace, lips pursed in a silent 'o' for the downed man's bruised privates. As I neared, he looked at me askance.

I shrugged. It was an accident. Really.

* * * * *

After class, we walked hand-in-hand into the pizza place to pick up our dinner—one large pie, light on sauce, one half topped with hot peppers for Chen and the other half dotted with mushrooms for me. Yum.

While they boxed our order, the monosyllabic teenager behind the counter picked at a zit the size of Montana sprouting atop his small nose. Chen and I shared a look that said 'Ew' and

I recall fervently praying those teenybopper hands hadn't been anywhere near dough or toppings.

A young girl brought our pizza to the counter. Her blond hair swung in a lopsided ponytail and her nametag read 'Hi, I'm the Asst. Manager!' Perky. She looked at me while scooting the box our way and tilted her head a bit in question.

"Aren't you the woman in the paper?" she asked.

"Paper?" I chirped, playing dumb. I shook my head. "No, you've got the wrong person."

"Oh, sorry." She pulled a newspaper from below the counter and pointed to my picture. "It's just that, see, it looks exactly like you."

I squinted. "Gosh, that woman's gorgeous!" I laughed. "I'm flattered you think there's a resemblance." I lifted the pizza box. "Have a nice day."

Chen held open the restaurant's door for me and in the parking lot, across the hood of his shiny blue BMW, my cheeky grin met his knowing smirk. We climbed inside and drove three blocks to his loft.

Chen lives downtown off Main and Fourth in an old office building newly revamped into large flats. It's a great location and that night I was eager to see his loft's interior. You can always tell a lot about someone by where they choose to live, how they decorate, the art on their walls, if they're messy or neat. I expected Chen's tastes to be simple bordering on minimalist because of his personality—it's quiet and careful, nothing extraneous.

Other guys, two months into dating, would have long since put the moves on me. I'd have been invited home by the second or third date, if not the very first. Not so Chen. He's thoughtful, deliberate. I like that about him.

After class, I followed him home to have my own vehicle later, part independence, part convenience. We immediately jumped into his car to fetch dinner. He parked beside my Jeep and held open the passenger door for me. We shared a smile and he took the pizza box as I slid from the car.

"What floor do you live on?"

"The sixth. There are two lofts per floor."

We took the elevator and he motioned me in first. I stood just inside the doorway and looked around an open, spacious loft, with soaring ceilings and exposed vents and pipes. Industrial. Even though my preferences lean toward traditional, I liked it.

I spun toward him. "Wow, it's terrific."

He smiled. "Glad you like it. I hoped you would." He took my hand. "Ready for the grand tour?"

The pizza plopped on the kitchen table and he led me through his home, quietly narrating like an eager docent. The furnishings were neutral, tone-on-tone beige, and gave the overall impression of sleek but not stark.

We looked out his bank of floor-to-ceiling windows. The view was one of busy people and cars rushing by, storefronts, treetops newly leafed, and blazing in the distance, a setting orange sun.

I looked up at him and met his warm gaze, brown eyes flecked with gold. "I'm impressed. Hungry too." I tugged on his hand. "C'mon, let's eat."

Chapter 6

We sat close on his couch after dinner, two glasses of white wine on the coffee table.

"What did you think of your opponent in class today?" Chen asked.

I snorted. "Not much. He was impatient…and far too aggressive." I wrinkled my nose. "Arrogant."

He smiled at my assessment. "Why do you think I paired him with you?"

"Wanted to teach him a lesson, huh?"

Chen played with my hair before answering, a habit he'd developed by our third or fourth date. He rolls one of my curls around his index finger and pulls lightly.

"A lesson, yes." His lips twisted. "But not quite the one he learned."

"Hey, it was an accident," I objected. "My foot slipped." And I smiled at Chen's expression, laden with teasing doubt. "He'll be okay."

"In a year or two perhaps, after extensive physical therapy."

"Har har."

"So…work. Tell me more about your latest case. Must be an interesting one to land your picture on page one."

Though I never use actual names of clients, I often talk to Chen about work because he's interested and asks. "It's an adultery case. Last night I followed the cheating swine to his hotel tryst." I flashed a mean grin at Chen. "And it was pure fluke that I wound up riding a purse snatcher's back. The whole thing was blown out of proportion—not even hit the papers if it didn't involve the mayor."

"Well, if it means anything, I'm proud of you." He continued to stroke my hair.

"It means a lot, thanks."

He cleared his throat, lowered and softened his voice. "Something's been on my mind for awhile. I'd...I'd like to talk to you about it."

He acted tentative, unsure, and so unlike himself, worry immediately swirled around my gut, clenching hard. I hoped it wasn't a 'I really like you, *but*' type of something on his mind. Heat stained my cheeks—anger or embarrassment, who knew? Probably both.

Chen was the first guy in quite a while I wanted to date more than once. Admittedly, sparks didn't fly in our relationship (at least on my end); I likened it more to an electric blanket, warm and comfortable, but we have many things in common and just enough differences to make for an interesting couple. Or so I thought.

I stalled by sipping my wine in the hope it might clear my head, or perhaps fuzz it more. Neither occurred. Chen watched me and, setting down my glass, I met his eyes. "Are you dumping me?"

He looked horrified. "God, no!"

"Oh, okay, good." Tension left my shoulders. "What is it then?"

He cleared his throat. "Don't answer right now, but I'd like you to consider our relationship an exclusive one. I don't want to date anyone else...and I hope you might feel the same." He swallowed. "Will you consider it?"

I saw such vulnerability on his handsome face and my gut clenched again, this time for an entirely different reason. I wasn't sure why, but it felt sweet and nice.

With a smile I said, "I'll consider it."

Gaze steady on my mouth, Chen leaned in closer to murmur, "There's something on your lips." Ew. As a mental image flashed of congealed mozzarella cheese, he smiled and added, "Me." Funny.

He kissed me.

My hands moved to his hair and he delved deeper, tongue rubbing tongue. Chen likes to kiss unhurried, measured, to feel each incremental touch and build the fire slowly. I was game. Absolutely.

His right hand smoothed up my thigh, and as it inched a slow path north over hip and waist, I remember thinking *Finally*.

He cupped my breast.

I leaned into his touch and as he gently squeezed, molding his fingers around my shape, the hum of his refrigerator caught my attention. In the quiet of his loft it sounded loud and sporadic, as if misfiring. Chen moaned into my mouth and the sound yanked back my focus.

His fingers brushed against my nipple before pinching through the linen of my dress, the lace of my bra. The sensation felt quite pleasant. *Pleasant?* My mind taunted, shouldn't his touch feel more than just *pleasant?* I swatted the thought away and doubled my attention.

Chen tore his lips from mine, his gaze searching me with heat and a kind of intensity I'd never before seen on his face, then his gaze dropped to his hand on my breast. His fingers moved aside and he took my covered nipple inside his mouth.

A car drove by on Main with obvious muffler issues and I caught myself distracted, looking out the window. Damn. Chen did everything right that evening, the problem lay with me. Swamped with guilt, I threaded my fingers through his hair, and as I pressed my lips against the silky strands, so black they shone blue, the telephone's ring pierced the moment.

We stilled and after the third ring, the answering machine broadcasted a man's anxious voice. The agitated tone echoed in the loft's open layout.

"Sounds important. Better get that," I whispered.

Chen sighed against my breast, raised his head. "Sorry. It's my dad."

While he talked on the phone, I straightened my dress and sipped wine, looking up when he set down the receiver. "His car stalled about a mile south. The tow truck's taking him to the garage. I'm sorry, but I need to pick him up. My mom's out of town and he has no one else to call."

"Oh, no problem." I stood and he met me halfway.

"You're sure?" His hands smoothed along my arms.

"Absolutely," I reassured. "Call me if you need any help, 'kay?"

He framed my face and kissed me again.

We rode the elevator down and parted ways in the parking lot, Chen going south and me north.

About a mile from home I pulled over for gas, regular unleaded, seven cents cheaper per gallon than the station down the street. Cost conscious, that's me.

I went inside for a pack of gum and the clerk just stared at me. And stared at me some more. I looked down at myself, wondering if I was buttoned up all neat and tidy. I was; nothing hung out. My light spring jacket fully covered my dress and the dark, wet spot over my breast.

I waved the gum and a dollar in his face.

"Hey, ain't you the lady in the paper today?"

"Nope." I waved the dollar more forcefully.

"Yes you are," and reaching behind, he pulled the paper off the counter. "See," he said pointing. "There you are. That's you."

"No, it's not." I squeezed George Washington's face blue, madly waving the bill in the clerk's eyes.

"Uh-huh."

"Nuh-huh."

"Yes!" he argued and held the paper next to me for comparison. His eyes moved back and forth between us like an over-wound clock's pendulum.

I rolled my eyes and with a huff, tossed the bill on the counter. "Keep the change."

I drove home chomping my expensive spearmint gum, still muttering under my breath about good deeds never going unpunished when I stepped into the foyer.

"How was your date, Desy?"

The disembodied voice floated masculine, silky, French accent. I knew to whom it belonged, question was, did I feel up to conversing with it right then? Not really. That night's master plan involved scented hot water and I frowned when the sweet image of a bubble bath burst, swirling fast down the drain. My wet tete-a-tete with Mr. Bubble would have to be postponed. Shame, we're great friends.

"Where are you?" I asked, moving through the living room.

"Library."

I made my way there, leaned against the doorframe and crossed my arms before saying hello.

The library, small and inviting, holds only two chairs, both deep and overstuffed; each flanked with its own floor lamp. The back wall is filled with built-in shelves overflowing with books — most of them on gardening. My aunt and I love to dig in dirt and watch things grow. The tangy scent of lemon oil reached me and I knew Aunt P had cleaned earlier.

With an open book on his lap, Armand sat watching me. He looked like a model selling books. Or sex. Or sexy books.

"Your date — how was it?"

It needled me for some reason that he even asked. His question felt more prurient than polite, his tone slightly challenging, and he wore that damn smile again, the one that says he knows something, has one up on you. I wanted to wipe it right off his smug, unbelievably handsome face. Anger flared; I vibrated with it. No good reason, but that's a woman's prerogative, right? Or is it just to change our minds? I always get that confused.

"It was great, Armand," I practically purred, steaming mad. "We shared a romantic dinner, then rolled all over the couch together. He was sucking on my breast." I actually cupped myself and squeezed. "This one, here, when the phone rang." My sigh gusted nice and heavy, full of regret, before I crossed my arms again. "We had to cut the date short, unfortunately. I'm seeing him next week, maybe sooner, though. I don't know if I can wait that long."

His eyes blazed and I got my wish—his cocky smile disappeared, wiped clean off his face like an eraser against a chalkboard—before he launched from the chair and stalked to me in four long, coiled strides.

"If you're in such need, just ask." His words were thrown at me like little knives, biting, his accent thicker, his tone dark and strained.

I made to turn and leave, more than slightly embarrassed, already regretting my rash words and actions, but he caught my arms and pinned them up against the wall, half-shoving me backwards. His dark head bent and he sucked on the same breast Chen had not an hour before. While his mouth and tongue worked, Armand watched me and the sensation was unbelievable, one I'd liken to biting into the nugget center of a Snickers bar, only better. That's quite a compliment. I love Snicker bars. Hands down they're my favorite. No question.

Happy chills raced down my back, the crotch of my new panties grew damp, and I stood horrified, aroused, and steaming mad all at once. Mad won.

"Stop."

Unbelievably he did, and straightening, gazed at me with burning eyes turned black with emotion. His chiseled features were sensual and hard, jaw clinched tight with anger matching mine. Goody.

"Let me go."

His hands tightened, then released. I stood frozen, shaking. He closed his eyes, inhaled deep and slow, calming himself, taking back what he'd lost—control. Armand's eyes slowly opened, lashes fanning inky and nearly longer than my own, and surprisingly, he framed my cheeks tenderly, pressed soft, open-mouthed kisses along my face. He murmured words in French and dived into my mouth.

I let him. Even participated.

The man could kiss—every one of my nerve endings told me so—and breath slammed from my lungs in a startled gasp when his hand slipped under my dress, skimmed a slow burning path up my thigh.

I wanted it there, wanted to feel his hand on me, cupping, rocking, his fingers in me, probing. I wanted to slide his zipper down and curl my hand around his cock. Wanted to plunge my mouth over it and feel his hard length gliding back and forth, straining between my lips. I wanted to feel his hands bury in my hair while I savored cream spurting thick and hot down my throat. Wanted to feel him thrust. Wanted to hear him groan. I burned with wants.

Shaken, I tore my mouth away and covered his hand with mine. "No."

"You want me."

Duh! I shook my head and half-snorted. "I want world peace too, but let's face it, what're the odds?" Dizzy, I pushed from him and backed into the hall.

I felt so utterly baffled—never before had arousal and anger twined together and filled me at once, like diving into an erupting volcano. And he was a complete stranger! I couldn't even remember his last name, for god's sake, or my own.

My hand moved to my mouth and through trembling fingers I whispered, "What just happened?"

"What is meant, *mon* Desy."

Now, when he said that, I should have replied, "What the hell does that mean?" or "Right, you nut job, pack your bags and catch the next flight back to gay Paree." But did I? No. It's just that tiny problem with hindsight again. Gets me every time. It would have been smart, but smart had left the building—it was the first of my many fine attributes to skitter away when he began kissing me. I was left with dumb shock. You can't do much with that.

I mumbled goodnight and clomped down the hall with curled toes.

Armand's smooth voice called, "Tomorrow evening, *mon chou*. Dinner."

Like I'd forget.

I climbed the stairs, unsettled and confused layered thick over mad and aroused, and I realized something. My mouth was empty.

The thieving bastard stole my gum.

Chapter 7

That night's imaginings began with forbidden fruit and a milk product.

Snug in my bed, my eyes had barely closed when the illusion enveloped me in bright colors, scents and sound, the vision crisp, lucent, so clear it was tangible.

A hot summer's eve, happiness and solitude my two companions, I sat nude at the kitchen table nibbling on fresh strawberries dipped in smooth whipped cream. The room's air scorched my skin, almost blistering, transforming each bite of chilled fruit into a sharp explosion before it slid down my throat in a startling, wondrous glide.

Sitting around nude? (Highly doubtful.) Hot enough that sweat slicked my skin? (Snow dotted my lawn.) Eating strawberries? (I'm allergic.)

I sat within my own skin, pragmatic enough to realize the scene before me no more than a simple nighttime indulgence, mere slumbering fantasy, though my heart still thundered when Armand entered the room. He wore only a slight smile.

The fruit sat forgotten on my tongue while my eyes widened, devouring him. It was impossible to conjure a more devastating man. His presence turned the room's already hot air volcanic, and in one blazing millisecond, shoved my sleeping libido into a steaming inferno.

Shining hair brushed his shoulders and I watched his pupils darken with bold promises. His mouth—those sensual lips—drew my gaze as their curve deepened into a full wicked smile. My stare dropped to tarry over his chest, firm and swirled with dark coiled hair, before slipping to his tight stomach. Rising from a nest of dark brown curls above a tightly drawn sac, reaching just past his navel, swelled his cock: thick, straight, coursed with veins and capped with a smooth plum head. A bead of pre-come shimmered there, nestled in his slit, tempting me.

I licked my lips, dragged my gaze from it, tracing back up his chest and face to meet his vivid eyes, and drowned there a full minute before I managed speech. "Fancy meeting you here."

His brow arched. "You sound surprised," he said. "Were you expecting someone else?"

"I wasn't expecting anyone."

"*Au contraire*. I'm here because you want me to be."

"Is that so?"

"*Oui*, and I would be quite upset if you dreamt without me. We belong together. Your consciousness denies it even as your subconscious accepts it."

My forehead knit. "That's a little too Zen for me to follow."

He strolled toward me, hips level with my head, and with each step I watched his cock sway. I quickly became dizzy.

"Watch the flagpole there," I cautioned. "You could hurt someone with that thing."

His brow arched again. "Flagpole?"

"Hey, it's a dream," I explained with a shrug. "I can say whatever I want." I motioned toward his lower anatomy. "Your appendage is very, um, impressive, but you could poke out my eye."

"That's not quite what I had in mind."

He stopped inches from me. I swallowed. "Well, accidents happen. Otherwise, we wouldn't need OSHA, or hospital burn units, or—"

"Desy?"

I stared at his cock. "Hmmm?"

"Up here."

"Oh!" My gaze leapt to meet his laughing eyes.

"You're adorable when you're rattled," he said.

"I'm not rattled."

"*Non?*" His hands spanned my waist. Plucking me up, he set me on the table's edge and nuzzled my ear before whispering, "Rattled yet?"

I shivered. "N…no."

Armand nudged apart my legs with his hips, hands still burning against my waist, thumbs circling, stroking just below my breasts. He licked the rim of my ear. One hand left me to return with a plump strawberry and, holding it aloft, he bit its tip. He watched me…and I watched his lips move as he chewed, his Adam's apple bob with his swallow.

"Mmm. It tastes almost as good as you."

My gaze leapt to his. "Me?"

"*Oui.*" Armand trailed the berry over my shoulder and down the swell of my breast, circling my nipple with a slow, tortuous glide. I gasped at the coolness, and with a smile he asked, "Rattled?"

I shook my head.

He lightly squeezed the fruit, bathing my nipple in its sticky juice. Droplets fell, splattering cold on my thigh before rolling down my leg in a frosty trickle. Breasts heavy, tips pointed and aching, I clutched at the table.

The strawberry trailed to my other breast where he circled the nipple, round and round and round, spreading sweet red juice, dripping it, until my entire body quaked.

I jerked when cool juice dribbled in my pubic hair, moaned when Armand pressed the fruit against my center, panted as he slicked it up and down my folds. A blend of juice dripped between my thighs, berry and arousal.

I cleared my throat. "Armand?"

"*Oui?*"

"I'm…I'm rattled now."

"Good. So am I."

"You are?"

Between my legs rubbed his slow hand, cold fruit, and wicked intent. His eyes met mine. "How could I not be? You're funny, strong, smart, and so...damn...responsive. You're beautiful, *mon chou*. Stunning." He smiled. "You're like this berry — sweet and tart and delicious."

With one finger, Armand pushed the plump berry inside me.

"Oh my god!" Shuddering, I grasped his biceps. Even as the fruit sat frigid within me, his body threw off waves of heat, the very air around us scorched, and a bead of sweat rolled down my back.

Armand rubbed my clitoris, flicking it with his smooth nail, nudging and pushing, stroking it, while moaning low and suckling at my breast. His teeth captured my nipple in a squeezing pinch and tugged. It was so lovely a pain, my eyelids slid closed.

With the chilled fruit inside me, a finger sliding on my clit, his mouth — warm and wet — sucking my breast, for the first time my dream felt truly imaginary. Nothing real felt that good, I thought.

He turned to my other breast and sucked, licking it clean, and my hum intensified to a moan when his teeth scraped my nipple. Fire lanced to my womb, settling there in heady, rolling waves, and everything inside me tingled and tightened.

Armand's mouth slid off my breast to kiss and lick down my stomach. Against his wet tongue, beneath my trembling flesh, muscles danced.

Finger swirling against my clit, he blew on my center, shooting tingles, icy-hot, to spear through me in loud echoes. I shivered, whispered his name, and Armand licked my outer lips, his flat tongue sliding in a hot pool of juice. When gentle fingers opened me, I spread my legs wider and felt his tongue plunge deep.

We moaned.

A fiery flush engulfed me. My upper body slid back to my elbows, and with eyes still closed, my head fell limp.

Cosseted within my heat, the berry warmed, softening, and swished about prodded by Armand's tongue. His finger strokes sped; my clitoris twitched and buzzed, readying to explode, and the strawberry lurched, tickling on its slow exit into Armand's mouth.

I burst. Red-hot darts pierced me and with a wild cry, I convulsed in hard pulls around his tongue. Captive breath whooshed from my lungs as my elbows slipped and I sprawled boneless, flat upon the table. My breathing slowed from pant, to languorous puffs, to one…long…sigh.

Expecting to see my bedroom, I opened my eyes. Above me sparkled the kitchen chandelier. I stared at it in puzzlement.

"I've never seen a more beautiful sight, *mon chou*."

My eyes widened; I lunged upright. Armand sat watching me, still, completely still, intent, black gaze burning with desire beneath lashes laying at half-mast. My breathing sped.

"Thank you for the strawberry and cream. They were delicious," he said, licking his thumb.

He hadn't eaten any whipped cream. My puzzlement fled as his lips curved into a full, wicked smile. He referred to my arousal, the cream he ate between my thighs.

I drew a catchy breath of surprise and smiled. "You're welcome." My gaze lowered to his cock, which pointed at me thick and straight and long and ready. I admired my imagination.

Armand rose. Three steps and he stood between my legs. "Touch me," he said. "I want your hands on me."

I could have started with his broad shoulders, rounded with muscle, perhaps moving to his wide, furred chest, maybe plucking his nipples before caressing my way down his torso, even dipping my finger into his navel. But I didn't do any of that.

I grabbed his cock. Wound my fingers tight. A deep groan rumbled from Armand, sexy and forceful, as his hips began to rock. Sliding within my palm, his cock felt heavy, stiff, smooth...exciting.

He stared into my eyes, framed my face, and leaned to kiss me, butting his cock's bulbous head against my opening. I groaned, wiggled closer.

Our lips met and the kiss rubbed wet and wonderful, slow and sensual. He angled his head left, lingered there, nipping, then right with languid grazes, unhurried, teasing, and left again, each time varying the depth of his thrusting tongue, the light brushing of our noses.

My mind wrestled with vivid images. I pictured smoothing whipped cream along his cock—sliding it back and forth from base to tip—sucking and licking him clean, Armand's hot eyes on me, seed spurting thick down my throat. But as we kissed, each poking tease of his cock between my legs woke a different image—his plunging cock stretching me amid a hot tangle of limbs and a never-ending kiss. I moaned.

Armand had his own imaginings. Without breaking our kiss or my grip on his cock, he lifted and carried me a few steps, settling me astride him in a chair. He whispered, "Ride me."

My breath hitched. I rose to my knees, my hand guiding his cock, and slid down his hot length, impaling myself. His mouth captured my moan before returning a deep masculine purr threaded with satisfaction and eager lust. Armand's hips lifted, but with a tight squeeze of my legs, I stilled him. "Don't move!"

He ran his hands along my thighs. "Problem?"

"You could say that." I gripped his hair and rested my forehead against his. "Don't look now," I whispered, "but there's a twelve inch iron pole wedged between my legs." His chuckle jiggled his cock and my legs clamped tighter around his hips. "Don't...move," I whispered.

Amused, he said, "Twelve inches? You flatter me."

"At the moment, it feels a slight underestimate."

He licked my lips. "And just how long do I have to remain motionless?"

"As long as it takes."

I smiled at his groan and in the next breath my body eased around him, loosening in acceptance. He hissed when I wiggled.

"You can move now," I said.

"*Oui?*"

"Yeah." We kissed and I bobbed on his cock, a slow drag up then an even slower slide down, over and over, while my hands dug in silk, threading through his hair. Armand felt huge and wonderful. Perfect.

Tongue swirling wet against mine, his left hand cupped my breast, swallowing it in a soft crush, while his right hand splayed wide and low on my belly, fingers burrowing through moist hair to stroke my clit.

With smooth glides, his cock filling and stretching me with each rhythmic pump, I was afire, inside and out, shivering in the heat. A delicious eternity passed, sublime, then on each downward plunge his hips began to rise and meet me in a firm grind, urging a faster ride. His rocketing tension was palpable, exciting, and my hips sped, flying up and down his length in bold, whipping strokes, the muscles in my thighs flexing, breasts bouncing, my body quivering near release.

He groaned and pinched my clit. Every nerve ending I owned gathered between my legs in a heady congregation and exploded. My hips jerked wildly and I soared, pushing a soft cry into his mouth. Tingling fire spasmed through me in swelling waves, tightening and releasing in a searing ebb and flow.

Armand groaned again, body heaving, cock twitching, and deep within me hot streams of seed pulsed.

His arms enfolded me and, spent, I wilted against his chest as our kiss softly ended. "Don't wake," he whispered. "Stay with me awhile." Thick and satisfied, his voice soothed me while large hands roamed the curves of my back and ass, massaging, gliding along my slick skin. Smiling, tired, I snuggled into his heat, burrowing my face against his neck, the brisk pulse there tasting hot and salty. He held me close.

And of my dream, that's all I remember.

Chapter 8

Know how sometimes you feel as if your day is slowly circling the drain? For no apparent reason? Well, as soon as my alarm clock shrieked on Wednesday morning, six o'clock sharp, that feeling swam forcibly through my bloodstream, thick and sour, like milk left out over a hot summer's night. The day hadn't even begun and a sense of heavy gloom hung over my head. I did my best to ignore it.

Don't tell any nutritionists, but I often skip breakfast, more from laziness than weight consciousness; still, that morning I made a point of sharing it and my many thoughts, both wise and inane, with Aunt P.

She's always up before the cock crows—says its just one of the many liabilities of old age. Sleep leaves her no later than four or five each morning. Ugh. Can you imagine? I'm not too keen on old age for that reason, let alone the thought of my teeth in a jar, terminal wrinkles, and breasts sagging to my navel. No, I like my sleep, consider it one of life's favorite pleasures ranking right up there between eating and eating some more.

So we ate our cereal—Special K for her, a good source of eleven vitamins and minerals, and Cap'n Crunch for me, a good source of tooth decay—during which I just happened to steer the conversation to the Parisian lightly snoring upstairs. I multi-tasked during the chat, pretending it didn't bother me he'd starred in yet another dream while simultaneously fighting off a blush with each glance at the kitchen table.

"So, when's he leaving?" I asked.

My aunt smiled. "Getting your goat, is he? Ruffling some feathers?"

"I thought we were discussing Armand, not farm animals, and no, everything's just peachy." I eyed her smile. "So, when's he leaving?"

"I'm afraid he didn't say, dear." She scooped another bite of Special K swimming in half-percent milk and talked around it. "Is there a problem?"

I sighed, munched away at the Cap'n before answering, and the crunching reverberated, making a happy sound in my eardrums. "I guess not. Nothing I can quite put my finger on, anyway." I lifted my bowl of sweetened milk, drank it down, smacked my lips, and sighed appreciatively. "He said he needs to talk to me about something. We're having dinner tonight." A napkin wiped away all traces of my milk mustache. "Any idea what it's about?"

My aunt took our bowls and spoons to the sink. She spoke over the rinsing water. "No, I'm afraid I don't." Turning, she scrutinized me. "You've always been such an inquisitive child. I love it about you. That's why you chose the profession you're in and why you're so good at it, but just this once, try to take something at face value." She smiled and counseled, "Enjoy your night with our handsome visitor without grilling him, hmm?"

I crossed to her. "I love you." We hugged. I stand taller than she does now. She's lost some inches with age, turned frail, breakable. I felt her bones under my hands and fought off the stinging threat of tears. She's so very important to me.

"I love you too," she said, patting my back, and I eyed the table. "Um, we wouldn't happen to have any strawberries and whipped cream, would we?" I said.

"No, neither."

"Good, that's very, very good."

She eased from my arms. "Why do you ask?"

I shrugged. "No reason."

* * * * *

54

Nick laughed. Full-throated, just this side of wicked, gusting deep from his belly, I've always loved his laugh and never miss a chance to provoke it.

"Okay, how about this one? Three men walk into a bar—"

His hand shot up. "Stop. Pass me one of those catsup packets please." Amused, he smiled and shook his head. I threw it a little wide and with ease he caught it one-handed.

We ate lunch in the office that day after spending the entire morning cleaning up files and finalizing the report for our latest client, Mrs. Lowell.

While Armand's tongue wiggled down my throat the previous night, Nick snapped pictures of Frank Lowell and his bootylicious squeeze, the lovely art major, Michelle. He caught them in action first at an outdoor fair locking lips at the ring toss and later, locking other anatomy farther south, at the Hill Top Inn, corner of 14 Mile and Walton.

Room 102, they'd left the lamp on low and drapes parted an inch. How remiss. It proved a piece of cake to capture them going at it missionary style. Seems our Mr. Lowell was a traditionalist when it came to screwing, but not when it came to keeping marriage vows.

We expected Mrs. Lowell to drop by that afternoon, and being the bearer of bad news and 8 x 10 full color glossies, I didn't look forward to the visit.

"How's Aunt P doing?" Nick asked.

I swallowed a French fry smothered in Heinz and fat gram guilt. "Great. She asked about you this morning." I speared another fry. "Said she hoped to see you again before she saw the shining white light and met her maker."

He winced. "No one can top her at guilt trips. She's the best."

Nick crumpled his lunch wrapper and after pitching it in the trash, topped off his cup with fresh sludge. Since the EPA declared his coffee a biohazard, I expected Nick to mutate soon, perhaps grow another limb or nose, and so I watched in sick fascination as he sipped the vile brew.

"Guess I better visit her in the next day or two, huh? It's been a couple weeks." I smiled and shrugged. Aunt P always got her way. His visit was already a foregone conclusion.

On his way back with coffee cup in tow, I crooked my finger and he stopped at my desk. I waved him down. "Bend a little." When he was within range, I used my thumb to wipe a little stray blob of catsup above his lip. What're friends for, right?

He stilled, caught my wrist and for a quick second, almost too fast to catch, emotion flared in his eyes before banking behind friendly, casual indifference.

"You had some catsup near your lip," I explained in a quiet voice.

Eyes searching mine, he released my wrist, straightened quickly, and cleared his throat before moving to his desk. We both pretended the moment, odd and uneasy, hadn't occurred.

Nick's never been much of a touchy-feely kind of guy around me. We hardly ever share even the most casual of touches. They make him uncomfortable. I traced the origins to third grade when he yelled to Tommy McQuire during afternoon recess that I had cooties.

The phone jangled and after its second ring, Nick rattled off our firm's name. A couple pauses and reassuring hums later, he confirmed our location and hung up. "New case possibly."

"Yeah? Any idea what it's about?"

"Missing person."

* * * * *

"And what do the police say, Mr. Reynolds?" I inquired.

"They say she's most likely just a runaway." His face hardened in anger and grief. "But they're wrong. Sarah's done a lot of things, but she would never do that. Something horrible's happened, I just know it."

The early afternoon sun, shouting spring and happy days ahead, spilled into our small office as Nick and I sat interviewing new clients, Mr. and Mrs. Reynolds, about their missing teen, Sarah.

She hadn't returned home after school last Tuesday and by six p.m., the Reynolds had called all of her friends and scoured the neighborhood. They'd found her car still parked in the school's lot, but no Sarah. The police made them wait the requisite 24 hours before filing a missing person report.

The reason the cops weren't Johnny-on-the-spot was because Sarah Reynolds, age 16, had a record. A long one. Mostly petty juvenile violations, a few misdemeanors— shoplifting, tobacco and alcohol possession, curfew violations. Not two months prior, she graduated from a Juvenile Delinquency Program.

That afternoon, I mentally sided with the police on Sarah's case. She probably ran away, I speculated; nevertheless, she needed to be found. Her parents deserved the peace of mind— she deserved a hug, and then a swift kick.

Mrs. Reynolds, a thin woman bordering on skeletal, sat tense and twitchy on our office's beige tweed couch. Since her daughter's disappearance, I suspected she'd subsisted on caffeine and air. Black hair overcast with gray draped to her slight shoulders and a blue dress hung sad and limp on her small frame.

Mr. Reynolds was an overweight businessman, tie-and-suit-manager type, balding, heavy jowls; skin tinged an unhealthy red and bloodshot eyes that bore misery.

Both parents were obviously heartsick.

"We appreciate the information you've given us." Nick tapped the thick manila folder the Reynolds had supplied. "It will speed our investigation. I think we have everything we need to get started unless there's something else you'd like to add?"

Mrs. Reynolds spoke for the first time; thin and limp, her voice matched her face. "There is one thing." Before continuing, she swallowed and darted a quick glance at her husband. "Sarah's recently been interested in the occult." Her edgy eyes traveled from me to Nick and back again. "She thinks she's a witch."

Chapter 9

Technically, on Wednesdays our office closes early at 4:30. In actuality, one of us usually gets stuck there far past that time. Since I had plans, Nick stayed put and hopped on the phone, managing to track down and interview most of Sarah Reynolds's friends that night. He also dealt with Mrs. Lowell; she stopped by around 6:00 p.m., long after I'd left. Lucky me.

Don't get me wrong, I'm not without empathy, I just disrelish ending adultery cases as much as I relish investigating them. Witnessing one spouse's entire life shatter and collapse is like watching a car skid wildly toward an embankment and having foreknowledge that the passenger inside will be hurt, and badly. At the confirmation of infidelity, some client's eyes tear, some simply glaze over in pain, and others deaden and blank of all emotion. None of these is pretty or easy to watch.

Life can be wonderful or a real bitch. I was glad to miss seeing that knowledge bloom in Mrs. Lowell's sad hazel eyes.

On my way home, I swung by the police station to get a copy of Sarah's missing person report. It was the only item not included in the Reynolds's folder. The mid-sized substation, Precinct 27, sat sandwiched between the city's library and central firehouse in a long row of municipal buildings. Inside is a quiet, near-sterile atmosphere filled with busy men and women, quite unlike the frantic hubbub you see on televised cop shows.

The officer I spoke with, one Todd Richmond, around my age—mid to late twenties—cute, single, immediately recognized me from Tuesday's newspaper picture and article. He took delight in razzing me about the whole incident, then took equal delight in flirting outrageously with me.

I flirted back. Figured it couldn't hurt.

Between smiles and sly but PG innuendoes, he opened up about the case a smidgen, letting drop the fact that the same week of Sarah's disappearance, missing teenagers from the county rose as a whole. Related? Possibly. Though the cops already played out the connection theory and came up dry, maybe I'd have better luck. Who knew?

He took my statement about the hotel lobby purse-snatcher and the process nipped less painfully than I'd anticipated. I've got a good memory and sight for details; the account went smoothly. One push of a computer key transmitted the finished report to the arresting officers and they'd contact me if additional information was required. I waved good-bye to helpful Officer Richmond and went on my merry way.

Reached home around 5:30 just in time to catch Armand sauntering down the stairs dressed to kill—dark beige slacks, black tee and lightweight sports jacket. He looked Fine with a capital F and smelled of expensive, woodsy cologne. The utter knave.

Equal measures of fierce dread and eager anticipation raced through me at the thought of time spent alone with the handsome Frenchman. At the forefront of my churning emotions stood the need to discover what he wanted to discuss with me. Curiosity alone made me keep the date. Okay, that's a lie. It was a lot more than simple curiosity but I wouldn't have admitted it even if you coated my body with honey and staked me down next to an anthill. I'd pit my stubborn denial against brutal torture any day. No contest.

"*Bonjour*," he purred, his voice smooth and rolling. "Your day at work? How was it?" Perfect white teeth sparkled at me.

I didn't sparkle back. "Work was just peachy. Oodles of fun. How's your day going?"

"Better, now that you're home." Suave. Too much so, I thought, swallowing an irrational snarl. He reached for my hand

and I casually edged out of range, rubbing my arms as I called, "Aunt P? I'm home!"

Armand filled the silence with, "She's not here. She told me to remind you it's bridge night with the girls." His intent dark eyes watched me. "We're not to expect her for hours."

"Wednesday," I said, and ran a hand through my hair. "I forgot it's her card night."

"Come." He held out his hand. "I have wine breathing in the kitchen. Let's share some before dinner, *oui*?"

I ignored his hand, less out of perversity than self-preservation. I didn't touch him solely because I wanted to so very much. Disconcerted, I turned in silence and made my way to the kitchen while French shoes treaded quietly behind me.

* * * * *

"Your aunt is a wonderful woman. I enjoy her company very much."

In the kitchen earlier over a meal of pasta, salad and wine, Armand was attentive and courteous, an amusing conversationalist. We discussed a broad range of topics—hobbies to musical preferences to sports and politics here and abroad. He was sharp and witty…and too damn handsome, with a presence so enveloping, I fought off overwhelming awareness and arousal throughout our conversation. I'd be damned if I discovered he was smart and funny, too. Life wouldn't be so cruel.

With a knot of stubbornness tightening in my chest, I chose not to continue the polite chitchat thing because I suddenly wasn't feeling particularly polite or chatty about chit. "Okay," I said. "We've eaten. We've talked. What did you want to discuss with me?"

After dinner, we moved to the sunroom. I asked the question as we sat; he surrounded by mutant flowers on Aunt P's garish couch, me on the cushioned wicker chair as the sun hung low in the sky, pouring its warmth and yellow brilliance into the windowed room.

Armand sighed. "That look in your eyes doesn't bode well for me, I believe. And here I've been on my best behavior, too," he said in a wounded tone. "I haven't spit, belched, or slurped my wine."

My lips twitched.

"Simple conversation, *mon chou*. For now, that's all I ask."

Simple conversation? "Nothing about you is simple." The remark wasn't meant as a compliment, but his expression, his slight smile, assured me he construed it as one. He would.

Armand objected, "You hardly know me."

I crossed my legs. "That's where you're wrong," oozed my oh-so-casual rebuttal. My lips curved before I continued and I admit the smile bowed mean in anticipation. "Armand Bellamy, age 26, single—never married. Owner of Merlin's Attic, a chain of stores throughout Europe that at last count numbered thirteen. You have three homes but your main residence is at 23 Gisame Park in the Villette District, Paris, France. You pop up in the society and business sections of the paper periodically and support a number of charities. Shall I continue?"

As I spoke, his eyes lost their teasing twinkle and turned serious, boring dark and unwavering into mine. I spent part of that morning surfing the net and making calls, curious to know just who slept in the guestroom, who I'd share dinner with that evening.

"No need. You've already succeeded in impressing me." His arms stretched to rest along the couch's back. "Though turnabout's fair play. Shall I tell you about yourself?" He smiled.

Oh, this should be good, I thought. "Tell away."

"True or false, you're an extremely competitive person."

Extremely? Well…I supposed so. "True." Score one for him.

"You love to sing, but you're completely tone deaf."

I winced. He must have heard me warbling in the shower the previous morning when I belted out a stunning rendition of Aretha Franklin's *Respect* in a piercing sharp flat. How embarrassing. "True."

"You have a sweet tooth."

"Peeking in my cupboards, Armand?"

His smile widened. "True or false, *mon chou*?"

"True," I shot. The score was 3–0. I refused to go down without a fight. "You love children. True or false?" I asked of him.

"True," he agreed. I surmised this little tidbit while researching his charitable donations, most of which benefited ill or underprivileged children. "If you couldn't be a detective," he said, "you'd choose police work."

An easy guess. "True. You've known money all your life— you grew up with it." Private schools and chauffeurs were written all over him in bold capital letters, large font.

"True." His eyes lit with something. Temper? Humor? Gas? I wasn't sure. "You're afraid of heights," he said.

How the hell did he know that? I studied him, grudgingly admitted, "True." Things I knew of him were fast running scarce. "Um, you're a neat freak." I concluded that from the spotless state of my kitchen after the two meals he made and the way he kept the guestroom neat as a pin.

"False," he said. "I make my share of messes, but never as a guest in someone's home." He tilted his head a fraction. "You love old black and white movies. When you were five, you wanted to be a ballerina and a fireman. You're independent, sometimes to a fault. As a child, you played with Barbies and GI Joes. Sophomore year in high school, your prom date stood you up and took someone else." He studied me. "True or false?"

My eyes narrowed. "I'm going to murder my aunt."

Armand chuckled. "Please, spare her life, it's not what you think. Over the years, she wrote of you to my father, and his will bequeathed those letters to me. I admit I've read them more than once." A hard look swept his face. "And *mon chou*? Had I been around the night of your prom, your missing date would have been unable to walk the next day."

I didn't doubt his words because for a brief moment, lightning fast, Armand had looked dangerous. Cold. Had I imagined it? I searched his face but found only pleasant amusement. "Although I admire your act of revenge that night," he added.

"You know about that, too?"

A smile curved his mouth. "*Oui*. Toilet papering his house was fitting."

A big grin swept my face. "I thought so."

We shared a laugh…but then he had to go and ruin it.

"You're never more beautiful than when you smile. You make a stunning picture when your doe eyes sparkle."

He'd said it all with a straight face, even managed to convey a look of total sincerity, which was no mean feat considering there wasn't a stunning thing about me. I felt like applauding. "And right now you're feeling anxious," he said, "because you're nibbling away on the inside of your mouth. True or false?"

I stopped the unconscious gnawing and voiced, "Game over." After picking at an imaginary spot on my shirt and stealing a calming breath, I met his gaze. "You wanted to speak to me this evening about something. What exactly?"

Armand stared at me for one long moment. "A word of caution, if I may. I'm interested in you. Very interested. And the more you pull back and run, the more I'll…chase."

My hands curled into fists. "True or false, Armand, you're *unbelievably* arrogant."

Armand threw back his head and laughed. A foolish surge of lust bolted through me at the rich sound. "False, *mon* Desy. I prefer the word…confident."

Yes, and therein lay the problem. Confidence is gained through experience and where women were concerned, he was obviously quite experienced. Too much so. He merely played with me. Toyed. Doe eyes my foot.

I stood. "I believe our...date...is over now. Thank you for the meal, it was delicious. Good n—"

"You've researched me," he said, cutting me off. "Tell me, what business am I in?"

"At Merlin's Attic?"

"*Oui.*"

It proved difficult not to smirk when I answered. "You sell witchcraft supplies. Although on your website, I couldn't find any eye of newt. For shame, Armand. I was quite disappointed because everyone knows when cackling witches stand around a big black cauldron, they're stirring up a steaming batch of newt eyes."

"Are they?" he questioned. "And what do you think of witchcraft in general?"

I sat with a sigh, tired of his stalling. "What does my opinion of witchcraft have to do with what you need to speak to me about?"

"Everything." He leaned forward and his arms hung loosely, elbows resting on his knees. "I need to speak with you on this very subject."

Surprise and puzzlement swept through me and lingered to crimp my brow. "About witchcraft?"

"*Oui.*"

"Why?" That one word held a wealth of speculative sarcasm.

"Because, Desdemona...I am a witch." He shifted and leaned into the couch again with a hint of a smile curving his lips. "And so are you."

Chapter 10

After a moment's silence, plump with astonished derision on my part, laughter gusted from me. I brayed like a donkey drunk on fermented berries. Snorted. Gasped. Doubled-over and teared with it.

Armand stood as I regained my breath. I wiped my wet face and eyes and caught his parting words of, "Your bedroom, the proof is there," on his way from the sunroom.

"My bedroom!" Anger propelled me to my feet and I scrambled after him. He'd already climbed halfway up the stairs when I cried, "You've been in my bedroom?!" I tore after him.

In the hallway Armand went first into his room and silently brushed by me carrying a black tote bag on his way down the hall. My door was closed; he opened it. "Hey!" I complained. "My room's private. You can't just go in there." But he did. I followed him inside, huffing mad.

Setting his tote on my bed, he moved to my dresser and gestured, "There."

My eyes followed his pointing finger to my small rock collection. I'd started it as a mere girl, around eight or nine years of age. The rocks now number 15. Some are polished; some still natural and rough, others hold bits of sandstone, mica or crystal. I collect rocks—so sue me. I collected them simply because I liked them. Nothing more. "What—my rocks?"

"*Oui*, and these as well." He motioned to my body oils and candles.

My hands landed on my hips as I fired, "I fail to see your point, *Armpit*."

His eyebrow rose to a fine dark arch. Lifting a rock, the one that shone with white crystal, he leaned against the dresser and crossed his ankles. "What did you call me?"

My finger stabbed his chest. Poke. Poke. Poke. "You heard me…and I want you out of my bedroom. Now!" Poke.

He smiled, thin as a blade, making his handsome features darken and turn grim. That was okay by me; I didn't care, nope. I looked grimmer. More grim than the reaper. The grim contest was mine—already in the bag.

"Your rocks are tools needed to cast spells, your oils and candles are necessary components to focus energy and call your power." He returned the rock to the small collection. "In the bathroom, there are flower petals and incense."

"Oh, for the love of god, those are just—"

"Necessary to invoke certain spells," he cut in.

"Listen, *Armrest*, you've snooped in my things and if that wasn't bad enough, you're now trying to make them out to be something they're not." I poked him in the chest again. "You're not a witch—you're delusional!" Displaying my best pitying expression, I shook my head sadly.

His lips twitched. "My little skeptic, let me prove my point through magic, yours and mine."

"Oh, goody!" I clapped my hands and jumped up and down, effervescent, bubbling with delight. "Magic!" I gushed. "Do you need a broom? Or, I know! I know! A hat! You can pull a rabbit out of one and say abracadabra!"

He straightened and chastised, "Magic is not a parlor trick." I watched him pull items from his tote bag—white crystals, seven in all, blue liquid in a slim vial, a thick white candle and a small bag of white powder or sand.

"What, no wand?"

He threw me a stern look ruined by the laughter glinting in his dark eyes and I batted my lashes.

Armand arranged his crystals to form a circle in the middle of my bedroom floor. He placed his candle in its center and where melted wax had sunk around the wick, poured a small amount of the blue liquid that pooled there, shimmering like a small pond.

When he reached for his bag of sand, I cautioned, "Not on my carpet you don't." He nodded his head, once, royally, as a king might to one of his subjects.

Armand removed his sports jacket and laid it on my bed. "Will you sit with me inside the circle?"

Does a duck waddle? I couldn't wait to watch him make an utter fool of himself. I told him, "Absolutely," and walked to his makeshift circle, plopped down inside with legs crossed Indian-style, and he smiled, settling across from me.

"All powerful witches have their own specialties. You're descended from Aphrodite and so your element to call is lust or love. She was also honored by some as the goddess of war. My element is a gift from Ares and has its base in war or aggression." His lips curved in warm amusement. "That is why our attraction is so volatile, *mon chou*. Love and war combined."

I shook my head. "Witchcraft, and now Greek gods, *Armhole*? What's next — leprechauns and fairies?"

"You scoff from fright. I would never harm you."

"I'm not frightened, you big French ape! I find this," I waved my arms, "pathetically amusing. Now, do your mumbo-jumbo-hocus-pocus act and get on with it."

"Very well."

He flicked his finger at the candle and it flared to life. I met his gaze over its dancing flame and arched my brow, figuring it a gag, just one of those trick candles, a joke. I was unimpressed. He turned his head toward the bedroom door and it slammed shut. That was no joke. Nope. I looked at my windows, checking for a breeze, praying for one; both were closed tight as a drum. Okay, I was impressed, so much so I drew a deep breath, then two.

He lifted both hands, palm up. "Take my hands?" Armand's voice rolled deep and soothing; his eyes studied me. After a moment's hesitation, I placed my hands atop his only to realize mine were slightly damp with sweat. How unladylike.

"Magic can be used for one's own goodwill but not personal profit. There is a difference between the two so tread carefully when casting spells never to gain from their outcome. Novice witches often struggle with this concept." He ran his thumbs over the sides of my hands as we stared into each other's eyes. "A challenge is brewing, Desy. It comes our way. When the moon is full, high in the sky, good will battle evil in witchcraft."

I cocked my head, half-playing along, humoring him. "Like white magic versus black magic?"

"No, magic is always morally neutral. Its practitioners are either good or evil."

"And which one are you?"

His lips curved into a small, indulgent smile and its warmth lit his eyes. "Good, *mon chou,* as are you."

"I'm not a witch."

"Yes, you are, and a very powerful one. Listen to my words: *I call to thee, once and always a part of she and me, help her see with new eyes and heart, the power within and of her apart.*"

A warm breeze glided around the room, whispering against me and raising my hair in loose ropes of curls. Armand's eyes turned pitch black, scary, and I made to jump up but his hands curled around mine, holding me there.

In a glow of fierce white, the surrounding crystals sprang to life and their shooting beams enclosed us within a brilliant shining circle. The sight was both beautiful and frightening.

My heart thundered. "What's happening?"

"What is meant. Try something. Use your magic."

"No."

"Don't hesitate for fear, magic is a gift. Try. Believe," he coaxed. "Open a window. Use your mind alone and command it to open."

Yeah right, I thought, not in this lifetime. "No."

"Are you such a frightened child, then?" he gibed, frowning.

The taunt got my dander up, but good. "Go to hell, *Armadillo*," I spat, and turned my head toward the closest window. I felt an odd prickling along my spine, like goosebumps and stabbing needles, and the air swelled around me, shimmering with life...energy...magic. It pulsed inside me, gathering power and force, and I said one word under my breath. "Open."

The window flew up so forcefully, all six upper panes of glass shattered, splintering to the floor in broken shards. I gasped and whipped my head around to Armand who watched me with a beautiful smile, as delighted as a proud parent at his child's first recital.

"Help," I moaned. The power still built within me, gathering strength. It hadn't released, but rather kept getting bigger and bigger, growing; taking me over, pushing me aside. It would burst, I felt, and I would be no more. "Help me, Armand." Shuddering, I squeezed his hands.

Concern wiped his smile clean. "What is it?"

"Too much!" I gasped. The wind's speed accelerated in my small room, circling wildly in harsh gusts and whines. It roared in my ears, knocking pictures off my walls, scattering papers from my desk, whipping curtains in a violent dance.

I had to target the power somewhere, release it, but I didn't know how. My moan built to a scream and the wind tore the wail from my lips, swallowing it whole.

With a look, Armand extinguished the candle between us, sent it flying across the room, and jerked me to him, crushing his lips to mine.

The wind whipped around us as I buried my fingers in his hair and returned his bruising kiss. We rose to our knees and ate at each other, tongues twining madly, lips clashing over and over, angling left, right, and back again.

Power hummed between us, flared and meshed. Burned.

Cries repeated in the back of my throat, growly mewls of protest, unsatisfied and greedy. I wanted more of him. Needed it. Now. And rage rose then, incredibly potent, irrational over the delay, feeling somehow petty and willful, but strong, so very strong, and it merged with my arousal until it became a burning, screaming thing inside me.

I felt combative, wanted to fight and shake him in passionate fury, squeeze him until it hurt. Bite. Wanted to see and touch him, too, crawl deep inside and lose myself.

I yanked his tee shirt from his pants and ran my hands under it all along his warm, firm flesh. He felt so damn good; it wasn't enough, though. No, the power riding me was unsatisfied. It wanted more, demanded more. I broke our kiss and ripped the tee from neck to hem in one jagged tear, tugging it from his body. Eager, shaking, ravenous for the flavor of him, I leaned down and with the flat of my tongue, licked one continuous swath from navel to throat. He grunted when I bit his neck.

My hands slid along the broad width of his shoulders, fingers tugging on his underarm's silky hair before caressing his chest, smooth skin shielding rounded muscle, threading through its light fur, then sliding across his nipples until they beaded to brown points. I sucked one and Armand's hands slid into my hair.

The more I explored him, licked him, touched him, the less the wind howled until just a warm breeze circled the room. Each moan rumbling from his throat speared and clenched inside me, feeding my magic.

With my tongue I traveled south following the line of dark hair. Broken French sliced the air and Armand's hands tightened when my tongue dipped below his pant's waist.

Power swirled around us, thrumming, spurring me on. Was it magic or me who wanted him so insanely? Probably both, I thought. The belt and button at his waist loosened with ease and the slow rasp of his zipper shot tingles to my womb. My mouth on the hard plane of his belly, dark hair teasing my lips, I peeled down his pants.

Past the elastic waistband of his underwear peeked two inches of cock capped by a smooth, heart-shaped head overflowing with dewy arousal. I lapped it clean. Armand jerked, swore, and clenched his hands in my hair.

I grabbed two handfuls of taut, masculine buttock and squeezed before edging my fingers around his underwear's elastic rim and pulling down. It puddled with his pants around his knees.

His cock sprang free, swelling thick and long with a straining weight that pulled away from his stomach to point straight at me.

A curious thought flitted by — that nude, Armand looked exactly as I'd dreamt him. Exactly. Magic, though, allowed no time for contemplation as it prodded me onward.

I wound my hand around him, fingers unable to meet around the thick girth, and felt him buck within my palm. My tongue traced a thick vein up his smooth length, and I took his stiff rounded thickness deep into my mouth and sucked.

Armand shuddered, yelled, *"Mon Dieu!"* Noises rumbled from his throat, deep and pleasure-filled, as my mouth slid up and down his cock in wet, slick exploration. He rasped my name when I reached between his legs and massaged his balls, rolling their full, drawn weight within his sac.

His breath labored; I heard it over the soft wind, and he pumped his hips in bold thrusts, brushing his cock along the roof of my mouth, sliding it along the full length of my tongue to the far recess of my throat in smooth, rocking glides. He cupped the back of my head, cradling me against him, and moaned again, louder still.

Between his spread thighs, my curious fingers traced a path to his anus. I rubbed the puckered entrance round and round, slipped one fingertip inside to caress the interior rim, rife with nerve endings. Armand groaned. My finger slid past the ring of muscles, pausing at my first knuckle.

Armand's hips stuttered, stilled. Voice sharp, biting, he grated, "Desy," using my name as a warning. I wiggled my finger and he stiffened, cautioned against further exploration by repeating my name in a tight voice.

I would have listened and withdrawn my finger immediately had not a telltale sexual flush darkened his body and his cock leapt excited within my mouth each time my finger moved. Torn, I wavered. Magic thrust aside my indecision, obliterating the last of my hesitation, and pushed me onward.

I slid my entire finger inside him. He froze, but his cock danced against my tongue. Wiggling my finger in the tight passage, I probed the silky walls until I found what I sought— his hidden gland, a firm swelling the size of a walnut, smooth and warm beneath my finger, and I rubbed it in firm, long strokes.

A shudder slammed through his body. Armand hissed, "Jesus!" and rocked his hips in wild, jerky thrusts with an unruly rhythm. In and out of my mouth his cock flew, lurching back and forth between my lips in unbridled, dramatic lunges. Armand's anus clamped around my finger and he shouted a stream of French, words that poured into the room with heat and passion.

His cock convulsed with contractions strong and robust as thick cream burst, spraying inside my mouth. I drank him down, seed and power both, and as the heady mix poured into me, my own magic, finally satisfied, calmed to a bare trickle of energy.

The light from Armand's crystals dimmed, sputtered, then died as the wind stopped.

His hips finally stilled. I gave his cock and anus one last stroke before withdrawing, and straightened to lock my gaze with his. Armand's eyes blazed black and in my hair, his clenched hands loosened. "Jesus, Desy." He gave me a hard kiss and leaned his forehead against mine. Hard puffs of air beat across my face. "Jesus," he whispered. "Where did you learn that?"

"The Discovery Channel."

A laughing sigh caressed my lips right before he kissed me. "Bed." He kissed me again. "Now." Kissed me a third time. "It's your turn."

I was saved a response. Aunt P was home. She called my name downstairs.

Chapter 11

Work Thursday was a nine-hour blur. Oh, I did my job all right, by interviewing in person two of Sarah Reynolds's neighborhood friends. School was scheduled for only half a day so I caught the teens at home right after lunch and although both were cooperative, nothing of value was unearthed.

I visited a witchcraft supply store too, Spells 'n More, corner of Woodward and Adams in downtown Birmingham. Not for me—the visit, I mean. Mrs. Reynolds mentioned her daughter believed in witchcraft and I thought it couldn't hurt to check it out…for Sarah's benefit. Research. Couldn't hurt, either, to purchase for the missing teen's case a reference book on witchcraft and the occult in general. I bought seven.

The rest of my workday? Couldn't tell ya. Just a blur, like I said. Nick gave me a string of odd looks. He knew something was up, even asked if I felt okay, and I lied, said I was fine. He knew differently but didn't pry. He isn't my best friend for nothing.

Feeling fine? Not hardly. I was continents away from fine. Entire solar systems away from fine. Galaxies even. No, fine would've been not having to call a glass repair guy for my bedroom window. Fine would've been not ever seeing Armand Bellamy's handsome French face again, or other parts of his handsome French anatomy either. Fine would've been if the previous night never happened. Used to be I had fine down pat…when I was normal. I'm not anymore.

I'm a witch.

* * * * *

The big bad wolf knocked on my bedroom door. He hadn't tried huffing and puffing and blowing it down but I figured that came next when he discovered I wasn't budging. We hadn't spoken since the previous night and like a turtle hiding in its shell, I didn't plan on it.

"Desy? You can't keep avoiding me forever. Let me in, *bebe*, we'll talk." He knocked some more. "Desy?"

Through the door, I heard his heavy sigh and departing footsteps. Ha! See, my stubborn denial won every time, I thought, but just as that smug conviction zipped happily through my brain, knuckles rapped again against wood.

"Moron!" I hollered at the door.

"Desy?" Aunt P said.

I cringed, swung my legs off the bed and bolted for the door. "Sorry, Aunt P. Do you need me?"

"Yes, sweetie pie." That's one of her pet names for me. It's both embarrassing and lovable. "I need help entertaining downstairs."

"*Armful* can entertain himself," I huffed.

Her lips twisted in a smirk before she could help herself. "Do you mean Armand?"

"Yep, that's the one." I crossed my arms against my chest and set my face in a posture that said 'I'm stubborn and proud of it.' She'd seen it before many, many times, and unfortunately, it never fazed her.

"Well, *two* gentlemen are downstairs." She turned and left me there, stewing alone, wondering whom it was. Stewing alone is no fun; it's much more jovial with an audience. I fixed my hair and makeup and moseyed downstairs to see. Nick sat in one chair, Armand in the other, and Aunt P held high court with tea and cookies.

She turned to me as I entered the room. "Would you like some tea, maybe a cookie?"

I declined, said my hellos, and sat in the small loveseat backing to the bay window, my arms hugging a fringed, needlepoint pillow like a buoy.

Across from me, the Frenchman lolled in his chair appearing so relaxed, I worried his DNA might unwind. And frankly, I expected to see that odious smile, full of knowing smugness gracing his too-handsome face, but it wasn't there. I almost missed it. Almost. Instead, he appeared thoughtful and a look flashed in his eyes I couldn't read. He stared at me for a moment, then shot his gaze to Nick. I followed his line of vision and found Nick staring at me, a teacup cradled in his large hand.

I cleared my throat. "So, Nick, I didn't catch you before I closed up tonight. Did you find anything useful at the client's house?"

Late that afternoon he went through Sarah's bedroom, with her parents' permission of course, trying to discover a clue. I was supposed to have met him if I found the time. I hadn't found it. Battling inner demons and the start of a massive headache kept me busy.

Nick sipped his tea. "As a matter of fact, yes, I may have found something useful—a diary hidden between her mattress and box spring."

I leaned forward on the couch and crossed one leg under me, sitting on my foot. I'd changed after work into jeans and a red tee that proclaimed 'Well, This Day Was A Total Waste Of Makeup!' Barefoot, my toenails flashed scarlet, painted Million-Dollar Red, Revlon no. 19, two coats.

"That's great news! Do you want me to go through it?"

"That or visit all her hangouts tomorrow. Which would you prefer?" He smiled, already sure of my answer.

I smiled back. "Which one do you think I'd prefer?"

Nick made to reply but Armand butted in. "How long have you two worked together?" he asked with dark measuring eyes. His tone rang contemplative.

Aunt P informed, "Oh, they've known each other all their lives. These two grew up in each other's pocket." She set down her teacup. "The times they've shared." She smiled in reminiscence, angled her head my way. "Do you recall the summer you climbed the big apple tree out back and were too frightened to climb down?"

I grinned.

"You sat on that branch for three full hours and absolutely refused to use a ladder." She shook her head. "No adult could coax you down."

"That's because she's the most stubborn woman ever born, bar none," Nick commented, his voice warm and fond.

"How did you get down?" Armand asked of me.

Nick said, "She jumped into my arms."

"And broke your leg in the doing!" Aunt P snickered before slapping her knee and bursting into laughter.

Over Nick and Aunt P's shared laugh, I met Armand's gaze. If I were to describe his look in one word, I would hazard *speculative*. Just thinking really hard. That couldn't be good, I judged. My eyebrows rose in silent question the longer he looked at me and I have to admit, he had the unnerving stare thing down. I wondered if he practiced it in the mirror.

The doorbell interrupted Aunt P's next let's-jog-down-memory-lane-and-embarrass-Desy story. Saved by the bell, I thought, and promptly popped up to get it, but she waved me down on her way to the door.

I was left with two men and an uncomfortable silence. Nick finally broke it.

"Did you find out anything at that witchy magic store?"

Armand straightened in his chair at the question while I studiously avoided his gaze. "Um, nothing really, no," I stammered, thinking of the seven witchcraft books spread on my bed upstairs.

"Magic store?" Armand questioned.

Nick's gaze swung to him. "Our current case involves a missing teenager, possibly a runaway. Her parents told us their daughter thinks she's a witch." Nick's mouth curved into a quasi-smile, the kind that's more polite than sincere. I swallowed hard as he added, "Can you believe it?" He set down his teacup. "So Des stopped by a witchcraft supply store today for research."

"For research," Armand parroted.

"Yes, for research," I said, feeling defensive.

"Look who dropped by, Desy," my aunt said. She reentered the room arm in arm with the newest addition to our quaint gathering.

"Chen!" I squeaked, pushing to my feet. He met me mid-living room in a warm hug, stroked his hands down my back, pressed his lips to my temple.

"I was in the neighborhood and wanted to surprise you." He looked from me to Nick, then Armand, and back to me. "Is this a bad time?"

Yes, definitely. "No, of course not." I led him to the men for introductions. "Chen, this is Nick Sage, my partner at work." They shook hands. "And this is Armand Bellamy, a friend of my aunt's visiting from Paris."

A cool smile edging his mouth, Armand shook Chen's hand, and then eyed me. "Am I not your friend as well, *mon chou*?"

I pushed out a little laugh, pathetic and weak, forged. "Of course. You betcha." I turned to safety. "Chen, sit with me. Aunt P is just retelling some of my most embarrassing childhood stories. You'll not want to miss the next one, I believe it's when I performed a triple Salchow flying backwards off the banister...or no, maybe it's the exciting yarn of one cold winter's eve when I sewed shut all the legs on Nick's pants."

"Desy," she scolded. "I'll just go and get some more cookies. They're homemade, Chen, oatmeal and raisin. I hope you'll try some."

"Thank you," he said. "I'd love to."

Aunt P started for the kitchen and the phone rang. She singsonged, "I'll get it."

Chen and I parked ourselves on the loveseat. I reached for his hand and he entwined his fingers with mine in a warm, reassuring hold on his thigh. Our sides pressed together from shoulder to knee, nearly seamless, but didn't continue farther, down to our feet, since I'm such a squirt and my soles don't quite reach the floor.

You would think silence a complete void, pure nothingness, but no, the silence in the room that evening held weight. It felt thick and oppressive, as did the testosterone levels, which were in serious overload for the room's dimensions, far exceeding safety regulations. My safety. I believe it's in the women's survival handbook somewhere and if isn't, it should be. No three males that gorgeous should ever be in the same room together. Never ever. Your eyes might cross.

How did it feel holding the hand of the man I date with fair regularity and diligently avoiding the stare of the man I'd seen with his pants wadded around his knees the previous night? Glad you asked. In a word? Scandalous, shameful, humiliating, appalling, and just plain awful. (So I cheated on the word count—trust me, the situation couldn't be adequately managed with just one.)

The men all sized each other up and I watched them do it. They all knew me, and I them, in different ways, and each knew things about me that the others didn't. The situation felt odd and unsettling. I wanted to bolt.

Eyes speaking volumes, and then some, their voices remained silent. I suspected one or two might soon start pounding his chest and grunting animal noises so I scrambled for something to say, yet failed miserably. My brain had flat-lined.

And frankly, I felt surprised by Nick's behavior. He does small talk really, really well, a good conversationalist, my Nicky.

That night, though, he sat uncommonly quiet. I don't know why. The situation could have really benefited from some inane chatter of weather or sports.

"Desy?" Aunt P said from the room's archway.

Relieved, I swung my head in her direction and saw she held a mountain of cookies on her best china. "Yes?"

"The phone's for you. He said his name is Todd."

Holy mother of god, I mouthed, rising. Three pairs of masculine eyes followed me from the room.

Chapter 12

Friday at noon was not the smartest day and time to search for a parking space at the local high school. Kids with new licenses hotrodded around the lot either showing off or lead footing it to the nearest fast food joint for a quick burger before fifth hour. It sounded like a car rally.

Still, after surviving the previous night's tea and cookie exchange, being surrounded by teens behind the wheel using permits so new the ink hadn't dried proved no real challenge.

I pulled into a dandy spot three spaces from the main entrance, lucky me, and walked through the lot with only one close call—a careening silver Jetta. The driver yakked on her cell phone and barely stopped in time. Tires squealed as loud as my heart and after I walked carefully around her car, she tore off without apology. Perhaps she'd choose Manners 101 as an elective next semester, I huffed, pushing open the school's door. One could only hope.

I stood in the lobby, tucked my sunglasses in my purse, and looked around. Felt old. Varied posters about student councils, pep rallies and cheerleaders made me feel several lifetimes removed from such things.

Signs pointed the way to the principal's office. We had an appointment to discuss Sarah Reynolds, though I'd arrived a tad early, roughly fifteen minutes, give or take. Her parents signed a release allowing access to her school file and so I thought I'd take a gander at it even though the police already had. Couldn't hurt. Policy said, though, I couldn't photocopy or remove it from the premises. Bureaucratic party-poopers.

The hallway forked and seeing no sign, I guessed eenie-meenie-minie-moe, and turned right, passing by the school's media center, teachers' lounge, and girls' bathroom on my way to being good and lost. Found myself there within minutes and paused outside the student cafeteria that buzzed loudly with voices and fresh hormones, smelling of greasy yeast and cheese. Pizza day, I thought, grinning, and peeked inside.

The sight was pretty much what I'd expected: segregation at its finest—long tables of cliques. The cheerleading table sat filled with clear skin and pompoms; the geek table with open books and packed lunches; the jock tables seated broad-shouldered young men shoveling food; and way in the far corner, past the band tables and the couples' tables sat the table of Goth. Surrounding it were ten to twelve mutant beings from a parallel universe.

I headed their way.

See, the picture I carried of Sarah Reynolds showed a girl with black, spiked hair, heavy eyeliner and black lipstick. Goth all the way. The two neighborhood friends I'd interviewed were just your average Sue and Jane. I rather thought these fine young men and women might be of better help with the case or at the very least, a good form of entertainment until my scheduled appointment time.

I pulled on a blue plastic chair and sat in their midst and they looked at me as if I had two heads. Conversation stopped cold. I filled the silence with a brilliant smile and Sarah's photograph. "Hi. This is Sarah Reynolds. Does anyone here know her? Recognize her?" I scanned their faces while I moved the picture around slowly. Two girls near me glanced at each other before looking down at their food. Interesting.

"You a cop?" asked the boy across from me. His fingernails flashed with pitch black paint while two silver hoops pierced his nose and a small diamond post stabbed his chin. Ouch.

"No. I'm a private detective hired by Sarah's parents. She's been missing now for over a week." I slid the picture toward him. "Do you know her?"

He looked at it and shrugged his shoulders. "Seen her around," he said. "I never talked to her."

I looked to the girls on his right, the ones staring at their pizza crust. "What about you two?" I pushed the picture their way. "Do you know Sarah?"

They looked at each other and the taller of the two answered, "Yes, but we don't know what happened to her."

"Of course not," I assured. "You'd have gone to the police if you knew anything." I scooted my chair closer to the table, leaning toward them. "When was the last time you saw her?"

"At school, the day before she disappeared. Look, we'd like to help but we really don't know anything."

"Okay." I slipped Sarah's picture into my purse and passed out several business cards. "Here's my name and number. If any of you do remember anything, anything at all, please call me." I stood. "By the way, where's a cool place to hang out after school?"

Goth boy answered, "Club Wicked. It's max."

"Never heard of it."

He smirked as if to say 'Why would you have?' Jeez, did I look that ancient to him? So obviously not with it? "It's a Goth hangout—music, dancing, things like that. It's over on Rochester Road in Oakland Township." He stood with his food tray. "I seen Sarah there a couple times."

"Thanks."

I wound my way through the sea of tables, heart racing all atwitter, believing I might have just stumbled on the case's first solid lead.

Did I have anything black and Goth-like? I wondered.

* * * * *

Highlights from the previous night replayed in my mind's eye as I drove home from the school. The phone call from Todd Richmond, the flirty police officer who took my statement

Wednesday, was just a polite warning about the mayor and his wife. They received a copy of my statement and intended to contact me soon to thank me, show their appreciation, yada, yada. Told Todd I appreciated the heads-up.

I returned to the living room in time to catch Nick leaving. He told me he'd man the office in the morning and go through Sarah's diary while I visited all her haunts. The man knows me well, understanding I'd prefer to be out and about than stuck reading teenage angst under fluorescent lights.

Chen readied to leave right after Nick. In the foyer he asked to see me Saturday night and, happy, I told him yes. He planned a maiden ride for us on his new bike, a Harley Road King Classic, two-tone silver and black. I looked forward to it and kissed him goodnight. Twice.

Left with Armand and Aunt P, I pleaded a headache and went straight to bed where I fell asleep reading about sorcery and witchcraft and spells and potions. Weird stuff, that; abstract, unreal.

I turned into my subdivision mulling about magic and about a block from home, my cell phone yodeled. The ID read Nick; he called from work. Turning my stereo down, I answered with, "Bambie's Massage Parlor, two-for-one specials this week. May I help you and a friend?"

"Brat," he chuckled. "Listen, I just finished reading Sarah's diary and other than the fact the poor girl seriously believes in witchcraft, the only possible lead I found are the initials CW. The last few entries mentioned them a half-dozen times. As in 'I'm going to CW tonight.' Could be a place or person. Any ideas?"

I pulled into my driveway. "CW—Club Wicked. It's a Goth hangout. I discovered from a student at Sarah's school that she went there more than once."

"What's the plan, Des?"

"Well," I stretched the syllable. "I was just about to call you. I'm headed there tonight and I wouldn't mind being on the arm of a tall, handsome detective if said gentleman was available."

"He is. Know when and where?"

"Not yet. I thought I'd do a little research on my home computer."

"Don't bother, I'll check it out from here. How about if I swing by at eight?"

"Sounds like a plan to me."

"Good." His voice dipped. "And about that massage, Bambie?"

"Ha! In your dreams, pervert!"

I hung up with his laughter ringing in my ears and slipped from my Jeep, pausing to admire the rhododendrons that stand clumped on the shaded, northern side of the house. Gorgeous, they bowed beneath the weight of showy purple blossoms. I'd planted them a few years ago as a surprise for Aunt P on Mothers Day. Made her cry.

I itched to walk the yard, discover what other gifts spring wrought, but nixed the idea because I wore heels. Three inches worth. Not the best footwear choice for walking on spongy loam.

In the house I traced a low hum of voices to the library, where Armand handed Aunt P a tissue. She sat crying.

My chest squeezed. "What's going on?"

My aunt's face buried in the tissue while the Frenchman's head swung up. "You're home early." His voice sounded as calm as if he sat at an intimate bistro on a quiet Sunday afternoon ruminating on current stock profits. I wanted to strangle him.

"Wrong answer." I knelt at Aunt P's feet and demanded of Armand, "What have you done to upset her?"

"Oh, don't mind me," she sniffed. "It's nothing."

"Yeah." I patted her knee. "When I'm feeling nothing, I often cry too."

Armand met my gaze over her garbled laugh. "I told her that your destiny has arrived."

"You…my destiny…what?!"

Aunt P said, "I'm fine, sweetie pie. Really." She wadded the wet tissue in her right hand, caressed my cheek with her left. "I knew this time would come someday but it still somehow took me by surprise." Her gaze swung to Armand. "Silly, I suppose."

"*Non*, only human."

I sat back on bent legs, resting my weight on my heels. "Alrighty then," I snapped. "Since I seem the main subject of this conversation, would someone mind explaining to me what you're taking about? I don't seem able to speak your language." Frustrated, my hands flew in the air. "If you have to, draw pictures, use hand puppets or Morse code. Something."

"She knows you've come into your power, that you're a practicing witch," he said.

I tried not to stutter my reply but it wasn't easy, every internal organ had shut down. Even my tongue felt thick and useless. I met my aunt's watery gaze. "You know I'm a…what he said?"

Armand sighed. "Can't you even bring yourself to say the word?" The wealth of exasperation in his voice made Aunt P grin.

"No," I answered. "I'm in denial."

"Denial?"

"Yes—denial. And leave me there. It's a happy place to be."

His lips curved in a small sad smile. "I'm afraid that's impossible. You're a witch—the most powerful novice I've ever encountered. Your time is here and you must prepare before the full moon. I'll help you." Lips twitching awry, he added, "We'll work together to discipline and control your craft."

I frowned at him and looked to Aunt P. "You don't think I'm some kind of…freak?"

"Desy, of course not! My sister—your mother—was a witch. Your father as well. They knew of your powers before you were born. I've always known you were special."

"Why didn't you ever tell me?"

"My father's doing, I'm afraid," Armand said.

My aunt stood. "If you both wouldn't mind, I'd like to rest." We made to stand but she held up a hand. "Please, continue your conversation. I think I can manage to find my own bedroom by myself." Aunt P gets a little touchy about appearing weak. I wanted to help her but knew if I tried, she'd probably whack me with something, good and hard.

I was left with Armand, the one person I'd rather have been skinned alive by rusty nail clippers than be alone with. Still, I had questions, ones seemingly only he could answer.

Chapter 13

I sat opposite Armand using the chair's arm to rest my elbow and prop my head in my hand. I studied him while he quietly studied me back. Before a staring contest ensued (one I'm sure I would win), I rattled off my questions.

"Why wouldn't your father allow Aunt P to tell me I'm a witch? What did you mean when you said my destiny has arrived? Why did my magic feel so sexually driven? And angry? What's all this about full moons and battles? And when will you be leaving? Soon?"

I frowned at his smile.

"Are you finished?" he asked.

I answered, "*Oui,*" to be cheeky-cute and petty and mocking and mean. He must not have felt any of that, though, because his lips curved up once again. If he didn't stop smiling at me, I would belt him one.

"Magic finds magic. You've been unaware of your power and birthright for your own safety."

"What am I in danger of?"

"Not what, but who."

I sighed. "Don't make me play twenty questions. Just spill it, *Armageddon.*"

He placed a hand over his heart. "I find the little love names you coo quite endearing."

I opened my mouth to sputter obscenities, vile and inventive, but found myself closing my eyes briefly and counting to ten, then twenty for good measure. "Armand, I'd love to sit here and banter about words all afternoon, I really would, but I have a life. Help me out here. You seem to have a good grasp of the English language. Use it. Please."

He sat relaxed, dressed in crisp blue slacks, a white shirt with the cuffs rolled up as a comfortable afterthought, and dark hair, nearly black, cast in a shiny temptation about his collar. The beginnings of arousal mixed with my anger and I tamped down both emotions, burying them beneath common sense and pure stubbornness.

"Your parents were high witches, a very, very powerful pair. They led the Wiccan council and as High Priest and Priestess, held rule over all covens throughout France. They were obeyed and beloved."

He spoke of someone else's parents, certainly not mine. My parent is Aunt P — I'd known no other. His spoke of abstract people in another day and time, unrelated to me, a fairytale.

Armand shifted in his chair and leaned toward me, earnest. "The council's members numbered thirteen. Power and birthright allow one to rule within its confines. That didn't stop Damian Bochere from applying when a seat opened and the council unanimously rejected him. He had the power, *cherie*, but not the birthright." Armand sighed. "On the day of your parents' death, you were in Penelope's care. The house, cars and staff were always under the safekeeping of advanced charms of protection. Advanced proved not good enough. On their way to a council meeting, your parents' car careened off an embankment and exploded. They didn't survive." Armand's eyes glittered. "It was no accident. It was Damian."

Aunt P had told me about the car crash, that it was an accident, but I heard everything else for the first time that day. I wanted to learn more and so like a good little girl, patient and obedient, I waited for him to continue. Still, the knowledge that my parents were murdered didn't cut as deep as if I had loved and then lost them. My parent lay resting upstairs and the only home I'd ever known sheltered me every day, a cherished haven. I felt blessed, not cheated.

In acknowledgement of my patience, Armand nodded. Condescension tinged the motion of approval, I thought. At least he hadn't patted my head. If he'd tried, he might have pulled back a bloody stump.

"My father was one of the high council's thirteen. For your protection, he sent you and your aunt from the country that very night. He bought this house for your safety and concealed your powers. Had you known of your magic, believed in it, you would have been found."

"Couldn't he have let me stay in France and just protected me himself?"

"*Non*, their enemy, your enemy, is powerful and ruthless. You were too important to risk."

"I'm flattered. So, this Damian, what does he want with me?"

"The council is no more, he's seen to that. He rules in Paris. But some whisper of birthright and the two remaining."

"Two remaining what?" I asked.

Armand's gaze seared into mine. "Of French birthright, only one pair of High Priest and Priestess remains. Damian views them as a threat."

I whistled. "Well, their days sure sound numbered. They'd better put their heads together lickety-split and stop him."

"*Oui*, I agree, but first the High Priestess has to come out of—how did you term it?—denial."

It took a second but as realization dawned, fast and dizzy like a roller coaster ride, I straightened in my chair and wheezed an objection. "Oh no! I'm not some High Priestess! You've got the wrong Wicca chick!"

"You and I, we're all that's left of the line—the only couple standing in his way."

"I'm not in anyone's way! We're not a couple! I don't want to be a witch! And furthermore," I huffed, "the good ol' red, white and blue is my home. I've never been to Paris...well, that I remember anyway. He can have it."

"None of that matters to him." Armand left his chair and drew me from mine. We stood facing each other in the library, our expressions mirroring in intensity. "I would challenge him by myself to spare you but I'm not strong enough alone. Damian's had years to hone his skills—I've had only one."

"Only one—why?"

"I was born a few months after you. Your powers were no secret; Damian knew of them. But my father hid my powers at birth in a concealment spell for protection. Everyone assumed I'd not inherited the craft. Not everyone in the same family receives the gift, like your aunt. My father's spell died last year with him." His hands curved around my shoulders. "Damian is strong. But you and I will be stronger. We can stop him together."

My eyes searched his and found only sincerity. "I'm sorry. This is not my battle." I backed away and his arms fell to his sides, hands clenching into tight fists. I started for the hallway and repeated, "I'm sorry."

As I left the room, Armand called my name.

* * * * *

I thought it would be that simple, too. Just ignore it, and it would fade away, like a bad dream—the kind you remember in vivid images upon awakening but by lunchtime the memory blurs and pales. Magic would leave my life, I assumed, and take all things mystical and French along with it. Problem solved. Gone. Done.

Naïve.

I dressed for the club, black, black and more black, Goth be thy name. Prudence reared and I armed myself, shuffled through my drawer of holsters till I found my shoulder rig, a vertical holster so slim it conceals easily under most anything.

My black sweater set proved no different that night, displaying just the barest bulge.

I own two guns and I know how to use 'em. Practice sessions dot my regular schedule. There's my Springfield .45 automatic; it has full power ammo. Great gun. But I was in a Browning mood that night, hi-power 9mm, and I checked its clip, slipped it inside my rig, and was almost good to go.

I added an ankle holster under my black jeans for double the pleasure. It's a snug fit and often rubs, but we'd be at Club Wicked for just a short time, so I strapped in my stun gun, high-powered, non-lethal. Tell that to the person you zap it with, though, as they writhe around drooling on the ground, squealing sick pig noises. And I pack a doozie—not the standard 250,000 volts, no, I went for the 625,000 volt model that costs more but drops your assailant flat in half a second. Makes a neato sound, too. At just six inches tall, it crackles and pops like a bullwhip. Pretty impressive.

My getup made me feel like a badass but alas, between you and me, I was a self-defense virgin. Sad, but true. (Although the week was still young.)

I checked my reflection once more in the dresser mirror and tried not to laugh at the surprising transformation when the doorbell ding-donged its happy greeting. The clock read 8:00 p.m. on the nose. My Nick is a prompt guy. I raced downstairs to answer the door but the sneaky Parisian beat me to it. He let Nick in.

"Hi, Desy ready?"

Before Armand answered, I replied from behind him, "Yep." Both men looked at me and Nick gave a long whistle. "That's quite a look you've got going there, Des. Did you do it on purpose?"

I grinned, happily ignoring Armand's scrutiny. "For your information," I used both hands to motion down my outfit. "This took me over an hour of hard work." A hint of black shadow played at my eyes. My lips and nails bore black paint, my clothes—you guessed it—all black. Goo more adhesive than rubber cement slicked my hair, the wayward curls tamed into wayward waves, and as a finishing touch, a nose ring, sterling silver, clip-on, clung to my left nostril. "I'm going undercover tonight. I think I can pass muster for a Goth gal." I met Nick's smiling eyes. "Agree?"

"Oh, I agree," Nick said and he turned to Armand. "Do you agree?"

Armand crossed his arms against his chest. "She looks *risible.*"

I mimicked his stance and stuck out my chin. "And that means?"

"I'll tell you tonight when you return." He smiled at me, full of stubborn intent. I glared back at him, choosing between firing off a nasty remark or a quick uppercut when Nick cleared his throat. My gaze shot to him and I watched his eyebrow arch. Right, I thought, time to go.

"Just let me get my coat." I pulled it and my purse from the closet. "Ready."

Armand snatched my hand and pressed his lips hot against my skin. "Take care, *mon chou.*"

Hell—those lips, that voice. I wrenched back my hand and stumbled out the door. We were off.

Chapter 14

I let Nick drive a couple miles before I asked. "So, why are you driving Anita's car?"

He glanced sidelong at me before turning at the light. "You think I would willingly leave my 'vette parked in a lot with teenage drivers?"

"Right," I said. "Stupid question." I scratched at my ankle holster. The damn thing had already rubbed the skin clear off my bone. "She didn't mind you leaving tonight?"

"Anita?"

"Yeah. You know, Friday night, just the two of you." My voice held a teasing lilt.

"No," he said in a dry, flat monotone. "She didn't mind."

Every time I bring up his wife's name, the conversation either sours or completely stalls. You'd think I'd learn. Time to change the subject, I thought, and perk things up a bit.

"So, I was thinking, if we buried him nice and deep, way in the back near the viburnum, nobody'd be the wiser. He'd probably make great fertilizer, too, a nice foreign additive. For the last couple years that bush has been off its bloom. Needs a little pick-me-up."

"Who're we burying?"

See, Nick just plays along with me, doesn't ask, "What are you talking about?" or give me puzzled looks. We've known each other too long for that, own a kind of verbal shorthand. I can be myself with him and enjoy *absolute* acceptance...well...almost... except for the witch thing...he needn't know about that.

"The French guy in the guestroom," I said.

Nick smiled. "I don't know," he hedged, "you have something going on there. I can tell. I'm a detective."

"Well, you missed the mark, Sherlock. Nothing's going on. He's a menace."

"A menace he may be." Nick passed a crawling Saab in the fast lane. "But when you two are in the same room, you can cut the tension with a knife."

"That's because he drives me crazy! He's overstayed his welcome. Big time. Seriously, I'm plotting his death. Are you game or not?"

"Tension, Desy…as in sexual tension."

"Get outta here," I huffed in denial.

"Cut it with a knife," he repeated.

Singsonging, "I'm changing the subject," I asked, "Tell me, oh great detective, what you discovered about this club. Amaze me with facts and figures."

He turned onto Rochester Road and headed north. "Club Wicked. Two years old. Owned by one Sam Bearns. Three stories of bass-thumping techno. Bills itself as an all-ages club with deejay music and in-house concerts. Caters to the under 21 crowd wearing black and doesn't sell alcohol."

"Hmm. Find anything on Mr. Sam Bearns, the owner of said establishment?" I asked.

"Very little. Late thirties, unmarried, lives alone—northern Oakland Township. No record." He changed lanes. "What's the name of that witchy store you went to?"

"Spells 'n More?"

"That's the one. Guess who the owner is."

"Sammy Bearns?"

Nick nodded. "Interesting, wouldn't you say?"

"I would, indubitably."

I saw a huge building up the road, right hand side, with flashing neon, two spotlights sweeping from its roofline, and a steady stream of cars waiting to pull into its crowded lot. Club Wicked, no doubt. I'd pictured it in a heavily populated area, say stuck between a two-star restaurant and an aging bowling alley. I'd pictured wrong. It stood all by its lonesome practically out in the boonies.

As Nick pulled into the club's lot, a parking attendant waved him to the right with a flashlight. We followed the line of cars and parked.

I shoved some cash, my driver's license and cell phone along with Sarah Reynolds's picture in the front pocket of my jeans. Stowed my purse out of sight under the front seat.

Nick glanced at me. "You armed?"

"Yep. You?"

"Yeah. Let's go."

We went. After hiking the acre lot, we were inside within minutes, and felt the noise and body heat hit like a hard slap. Nick and I paid our entrance fee, checked our coats and stood against the back wall watching the pubescent show.

Wall to wall bodies. Some at tables, some milling, some continually bouncing straight up and down below strobe lights on the dance floor (the new millennium dance for people with two left feet), or a dandy way to induce fluid to surround your brain. Glow sticks swirled, jumping wildly in countless hands while the deejay played the music at a volume so deafening it threatened to bleed eardrums.

I spied an exit at the rear wall with a lit sign and arrow pointing up for level two, and I grabbed Nick's hand, made my way to it, planning to check out the entire place before splitting from him to flash around Sarah's picture.

Two giggling girls teetered by on high heels. We trailed behind them down a short hallway and up the stairs. I found the fact that Nick hadn't freed his hand from mine surprising.

The music carried up, the bass still rocked the walls, but overall the volume blared about half so that you could manage a conversation without screaming. There was no dance floor, just sectional seating in long, curvy lines of flamboyant teal and orange. (Aunt P would've approved.) Video arcade games rimmed the room and a large food and beverage bar stood planted on the left staffed with two bustling men, college-age, filling cola and nacho orders.

I motioned to Nick that I'd hit the bar and he nodded, squeezed my hand, before moving toward the circular bank of video arcade games.

Pushed my way through the heated bodies and wafting pheromones to the bar, slipped onto a swivel stool and looked around while I waited, feeling privileged to witness the typical middleclass suburbanite teen's mating dance—girls wearing too much makeup showing midriffs with navel rings and boys barely wearing jeans three sizes too big trying inordinately hard to look nonchalant. I grinned at the sight.

"Take your order?" I swiveled toward the bar and its 'tender, a slender, smiling man with a stubby nose, spiked blond hair, spiked choke collar and matching spiked bracelet. Obviously he liked sharp, pointy things.

I smiled back. "Hi. This is my first time here. What's your name?"

His smile kicked up a notch. "Mike. What's yours?"

"Desy. Have you worked here long?"

He thought it over. "About a year now."

"Cool. Um, could I have two cokes? Large?"

"Coming right up."

I swiveled round again and spied Nick mixing with a small group of guys near the House of Dead shooting game. He manned the left gun and did quite well racking up bonus points.

Nick won't own up to this, but I'm the better shot. Yep. We visit the practice range together occasionally and I usually outshoot him. My aim is better, simple as that. Not that I compare or anything, no, that would be childish, unprofessional even. (Last time we went, I didn't stop crowing about my center hits for days.)

"Here you go, Desy," Mike said.

I spun around. "Thanks." Leaning left, I dug in my pocket, withdrew some ones and Sarah's picture. "Here, keep the change." While he flashed me another smile and thanked me, I slid the photo across the glossy black counter. "I'm looking for my girlfriend. Have you seen her?"

Mike studied the picture and looked up with a sheepish grin. "Sorry. There're too many faces to keep track of. She doesn't look familiar to me."

"Could I trouble you to ask your coworker there?"

"Sure." He checked with his friend. I saw them both shake their heads no before Mike returned the picture.

"Sorry," he said. "Tom hasn't seen her either."

"Thanks."

He tapped the counter to say welcome then moved down three barstools to take the next customer's order.

I slid off the stool and found Nick showing Sarah's picture to a girl off by herself near a car racing game. I joined them just as she shook her head, moved way.

"Here's a cold one for you," I said, handing him a coke.

"Thanks. Any luck?"

"Zippedy-do-dah. You?"

"The same. I asked about the third floor. Supposedly it's a lower level and off limits—only for VIP's. The kids said it has some type of high-tech thumbprint reader, so I guess that floor's closed." He sipped his coke. "How about if I finish this level while you canvass downstairs?"

I sampled my carbonated sugar and considered him. "Sure. Where and when do we meet?"

He glanced at his watch. "One hour, downstairs at the coat check."

"Okay." I took a few steps, turned back to him. "By the way, Nicky, do you have enough quarters?"

His lips twisted before curving upwards. "Yeah."

I saluted him and made my way downstairs to 100 decibels of earsplitting fun. Before entering, I detoured to the women's restroom. My bladder jiggled like an overfilled water balloon with heavy squiggly pressure, readying to burst. And golly gee, I was in luck—the line snaked only ten or eleven squirming bodies long.

Chapter 15

After dumping my coke down the drain, I threw away the empty cup and washed my hands. Above the row of sinks the mirror reflected a girl exiting the bathroom. It wasn't her black hair, short and spiked, that stilled my hands under the running water, but rather the quick shot of a profile that grabbed me by the throat and squeezed.

She looked like Sarah Reynolds. Couldn't be, though.

I raced after her with racing heart, wet hands, and no suspicion whatsoever that everything was just about to hit the fan. In dark gray pants and a slinky black top, she turned a corner, moving in the opposite direction from the main dance room.

Thank God for my black Nikes, quick and soundless, as I rounded the corner to find another hallway, mid-sized and straight, with her at the end pulling open a door. I called Sarah's name. Now, if someone shouted a name behind you, even if it wasn't your own, wouldn't curiosity swivel your head? Just a quick peek? She didn't pause. Not a twinge. Without the slightest hesitation, the girl went through the open doorway.

Undeterred, I sprinted down the hall and tried to catch the door before it closed. The sign above it read Restricted—VIPs Only. I saw the thumbprint reader on the right. Saw also the damn door closing. If it did, I was screwed.

With no other option available, I dived and slid along the tiled floor, jamming my fingers near the ground in the half-inch opening between door and frame. My head and shoulder made the unyielding acquaintance of the cinderblock wall—hello, nice to meet you—as I thudded into cement. Stars burst. The steel door tried its best to ignore my wet fingers and snap shut.

I groaned, skinning my knuckles as my hands squeezed farther inside the crack and, clamping around the thick steel, I dragged the heavy weight back open. Inside I stood and caught my breath.

Darkness surrounded me in what looked like a large auditorium. I ignored my shoulder — ignored, too, my head and fingers, all viciously throbbing; they hardly mattered. More important things were happening at that moment.

Like magic.

The room pulsed with it as if alive with its own heartbeat and soul. Power tingled along my spine and shook me, almost drove me to my knees. I sagged against the wall, so chilled my teeth chattered, and tried to breathe around the suffocating energy. My heart jumped wildly in my throat, and like a full pop can shaken violently, I felt I might bubble over and explode. Just burst. Splatter. A large mess.

Voices reached me in bouncing echoes and I heard many chanting as one over the pulsing roar of my eardrums. Shaky legs helped me push off the wall and stumble through the power toward the steel guardrail. I grabbed, clung to it like a lifeline, and looked below to watch the scene.

The problem? Evil swelled in the room that night. How did I know? No idea. My surety didn't spring from the deductive reasoning of a detective, that's for sure, so it undoubtedly arose from the part of me that's witch.

They chanted the same repeated phrase in a foreign language. My best guess was Latin, although I couldn't understand a single word, and perhaps they chanted about lollipops and sunshine, but my gut said otherwise.

The room was circular and concert-hall large. I stood in the shadowed balcony that circled the room's perimeter and viewed vacant upholstered chairs running in red tiered rows below. A circle of people recited their mantra around a large pentagram painted on the floor. A raised platform sat empty in its very center and flames from dozens of black candles danced, casting eerie light and shadow. Like the scene needed more eerie. Already had plenty. It was overkill if you asked me.

The circled group appeared an odd assortment of beings, all different ages. I spotted a man around forty sporting glasses and a goatee, two men I placed in their early twenties, one teenaged boy, standing tall and thin, gangly. The rest were young girls, teenagers all, thirteen people total. I searched their faces looking for Sarah and found her chanting with head bowed in supplication.

Was it truly her? I still was unsure. I needed a good frontal view, but in order to get it, movable limbs on my body were necessary, and that demand was too heavy. Just remembering to breathe overtaxed me.

The room swelled with the group's rising voice; menace beat at me. Heart pounding in my throat, I tried swallowing it down to its rightful place before I choked, but it lurched higher when a man approached the pentagram from the circle's darkened edge. A hooded black robe shrouded his form.

Proportions, that's how I recognized the figure as masculine: wide shoulders, large hands. The chanting ceased, and dropping to their knees as one, the group bowed low with arms outstretched and heads touching the floor.

Looked like the Grand High Poobah had arrived.

I felt my teeth grind together and stopped the tense motion with an impatient toss of my head, turning seriously pissed over my fright. A wuss I'm not. My lungs filled with large calming breaths of air, and I let each one out unhurried, even and deliberate, so that my heart slowed from beating madly — fluttering like a small, frightened bird's — to a puttering, edgy thrum, which was much more acceptable. Thrum I could live with.

Poobah guy paused at the platform. "Rise, my children. Let us begin." His smooth voice, a pleasant baritone, filled the room and on hearing it, a thought flashed that if the witch business didn't pan out for him, he could easily fall back on his voice; I'm talking announcer quality, radio personality, orator caliber. Though something bothered me about it—that voice of his. My mind only teased at the problem, just out of reach, like holding a piece of candy for a child, dangling it there, a shining temptation, then snatching it back. I couldn't push past my twitching brain cells exactly why it vexed, and so I tucked the troubling thought away for later contemplation, like when I had a functioning cerebellum.

It would have helped knowing then what I know now. Had I realized why his voice bothered me, things might have worked out differently. Hindsight again.

His followers stood as bidden and he reached for his hood. Now that I believed in witchcraft and magic, I figured vampires, werewolves and demons couldn't be that far behind, right? Stands to reason. And so in the back of my mind, sensing all this evil, I expected to see one very scary dude: two little horns, perhaps, jutting from his forehead, or at the very least, a sinister cast to his face. You know, doom and gloom, the boogie man. I braced myself for the unnerving sight.

He pushed back his hood.

My breath expelled with a silent whoosh.

He looked like your everyday Tom, Dick or Harry. Normal, with a face so pleasant, one might label it jolly. I was at once vastly relieved and gravely disappointed. Some bad guy he was! Mowing his lawn, taking out the garbage on a Sunday night, perhaps grilling burgers on occasion for his golfing buddies—I easily pictured these scenarios, no problem.

Late 40's, early 50's, that's where he fell. Nick had described the club's owner as being in his late thirties, so the Grand High Poobah was not Sam Bearns.

Sparse graying hair topped his head, thinning into a receding line. If he caught it in time, I mused, he'd be able to stop that male pattern baldness right in its tracks just by popping a few growth hormones. Ted, my neighbor, seemingly grew hair overnight on the stuff and had strutted around for an entire summer like a hairy peacock squawking about his discovery of the fountain of youth and new hair follicles.

Words were exchanged below in a low murmur and I had two pressing needs: to hear them and to see Sarah's face. With the chanting stopped, the power rushing through the room quieted. Not left, just dimmed, like lowering a stereo's volume from wail to hum.

I tested my legs and made the delightful discovery they worked. (Scared stiff is not just a saying, you know.) I unclamped my hands from the guardrail and crept downstairs. Thirteen against one were not great odds — I preferred thirteen against two and so I sent Nick a cell phone text message with a quick missive of '911-VIP.' Figured it couldn't hurt. If it *was* Sarah Reynolds, I'd need help and if it wasn't, I'd look a little sheepish with egg on my face. Big deal. It wouldn't be the first time I wore an egg facial.

I perched on the third stair from the bottom and crouched low (as in stealthy, not scared shitless), watching the happenings from a fifteen-twenty foot span. Only problem, the girl I thought to be Sarah faced away from me. The Poobah cut off my mumbled obscenity.

He stood before a lovely girl whose black shoulder-length hair framed wholesome features. Petite, with an appearance so honest you'd entrust her with your house or kids, she stared at him. Poobah's hand curved around her shoulder. "You," he said, and she walked without hesitation to the dais where he assisted her up, laid her flat.

I didn't like it — her lying there docile and silent, the very room itself or the people in it, much less the feeling in the pit of my stomach. All not good.

The folds of his black robe hid a pocket or two because he withdrew a medium-length-curved knife that gleamed wicked in the swaying candlelight. A scream lodged in my windpipe through sheer force of will...and the fact my nails bit into my palms. Pain, the great stabilizer.

I watched as he circled the platform three times, listened disbelieving as he intoned, "*I give you this sacrifice, my lord below; blood of a virgin, pure and fine; grant me power over my foe; for triumph and victory shall be mine.*"

That didn't sound good. Blood? Sacrifice? The room echoed with the coven's chants of 'triumph and victory' and over the prostrate teen, Poobah raised his knife.

That moment, just a split second, filled my body with shocked incredulity and cautioned that what I witnessed couldn't be real. It's the moment your mind blanks, refusing to deal with something abhorrent, and tries to shut down or make excuses. Rationalize. Like maybe I viewed a play rehearsal or just some sick game, but it wasn't real. Just sit back, it reasoned, and watch quietly from the sidelines, where you're safe.

The knife flashed once in the candlelight before he thrust it at her heart.

Chapter 16

I didn't listen to my mind, I listened to my gut, and it said if I didn't do something damn quick, I'd watch a young girl's life be taken and become an accessory to murder in one quick slice.

I screamed "No!" at full lung capacity. It rose over the chanting, the evil permeating the room, the eerie candlelight, and stopped Grand High Poobah's knife three inches from her heart. He turned toward me as I approached, but oddly, none of his followers moved. Like molded lumps of clay, they stood silent, unaffected by my earsplitting scream or presence.

"Who are you? How did you get in this room?" he demanded.

Three feet separated us. "I'm a VIP. Didn't you get the memo?"

Up close I saw all the imperfections of his lived-in face — the sags, the wrinkles, the flaws. He had one beak of a nose, too — large and crooked, topped by a lumpy center knot — testimony to a break unset. I pointed at it. "You know, I have a friend of a friend who's a cosmetic surgeon and he'd fix that little problem of yours in one afternoon. Strictly outpatient." I cocked my head. "Care for a referral?"

His lips firmed and anger twisted his jolly features hostile.

I shivered. "Um, I'm a Scorpio. What's your sign?" Pelted with enough inane chatter, would he forget to chop me into itty-bitty pieces the size of confetti? I crossed my fingers.

He pointed at me and I felt a surge of power, his or mine — wasn't sure whose — before he commanded, "Be gone!"

Like a shining bullet, blue light shot from his fingertip. My hands jerked up in that instinctive arm block you do to shield your face. To cap off that skillful defensive move, I yelped.

He flashed a smirk before the light hit me, and a frown afterward. I stood unhurt. Warmth, a small tingle, that's all I felt, and lowering my arms, I mirrored his frown.

"Witch!" he hissed.

"Sticks and stones," I sang. He pointed again and I sighed loudly. "Please, don't bother. I think you're just shooting blanks tonight." A mocking smile failed when my dry lips stuck in spots to my gums; I managed only to eke a sick simile, more grimace than grin, while the Sahara burned inside my mouth.

My best poker face and I nonchalantly sidled alongside his virginal sacrifice. The teen stared at the ceiling and I snapped my fingers. No response. Not even a blink.

My gaze swung to him. "What have you done to her, some kind of trance?"

Poobah's brow furrowed, puzzlement written on his face as easily read as a book, and he tried circling behind me but I wouldn't let him. Didn't fancy a knife buried in my back. "How could you block one of my most powerful attacks and not be able to identify the simplest of binding spells?" His eyes narrowed. "Who are you?"

"Glenda, the good witch from the north, and it's time for Dorothy to go home."

He thundered, "Enough!" Obviously no fan of old classics, he looked fit to be tied. Poobah spoke then in Latin or Aborigine or Swahili, all Greek to me, and I tugged on the virgin's arm knowing all the while it would be futile. It was. She was dead weight and quite unhelpful.

Grand High Poobah's voice stopped, and just when relief spread within me like a soothing balm, I heard something move behind me. Something unpleasant. Something unexpected. Something horrifying. I whipped my head around and screamed.

Hundreds and thousands of them poured from the walls. Beetles. Ugly, black, their shield-like shells iridescent and shiny, they streamed toward me in droves. Scurrying behind glass at the zoo, where they belonged, I would have oohed and ahhed. Unfortunately, they weren't and I didn't. And dammit, I was armed but with the wrong weapon—I needed a jumbo can of Raid.

I screamed again instead. Like that would help.

Poobah cackled as I sprinted past with Olympic gold medal speed. I tried to ignore him just as I tried to ignore the click and clack of hard shells rubbing one against the other, hundreds against hundreds, the swish of legs and antennae...along with the sick knowledge that I couldn't possibly outrun them.

I climbed the stairs, scrambling up each tread faster and faster. Looked over my shoulder and wished I hadn't. Not three feet away, they gained on me en masse. I screamed again and my hair flew in my eyes, a wild curly mess, as I sprinted up each stair. They came for me in an echoing, clinking rustle, six legs each, multiplied by thousands—it's a terrifying sound, a rattling pitter-patter that still visits me in nightmares.

Just a few short stairs from the balcony and exit and safety, I tripped. The throb of my shin was nothing compared to the roar of my heart or the piercing echo of my screams and cries...or the sound behind me.

Cool cement under my palms, I scrambled ahead on all fours.

Know how in horror movies the victim always pauses and looks back? And you think 'You big dummy, don't look back!' Well, I have the answer now. You have to be superhuman *not* to look back. It's an instinct, a stupid one I'll admit, but it's there all the same, forcing your unwilling head to swivel and take another gander at what's chasing you, no matter how awful.

I looked back.

The swarm's lead beetles leapt on my shoes and crawled up my legs. Some scrambled atop my jeans, prickling my thighs, while others crept inside my pant legs and scurried along my skin. Their hard, squat bodies crawled up me, barbed legs pinching, swallowing me, as I continued a mad scrabble to the door.

Each breath exploded with a scream, roaring in my ears, and large hands grasped my shoulders, shook me hard. I looked up, dumbfounded, gasping, to see Nick. "Sweetheart, what is it? What's the matter?" he urged. Kneeling beside me, he looked sick with concern. The lights were on and a stranger stood behind Nick, worry shining in his eyes.

My gaze left him to trace the line of my body, half-lying on the floor somehow, and down the stairs. I saw nothing. Not one beetle. Not one person. Zilch.

Nick smoothed the hair and tears from my face. "Desy, love," he said with great care. "Tell me what's wrong."

I lunged into his arms. "Witches. Knife. Beetles." I buried my face in his neck, hid it in warmth and safety, gulped Nick's familiar scent, and began to calm. Relief swept away my muscles, melted my bones, so that I melded into him.

The man behind us cleared his throat. "Mr. Sage, I think your friend has obviously had a bad reaction to…something."

Nick hugged me, glided his hands along my back. "My friend doesn't take drugs," he said over my shoulder.

The man sighed. "Well, perhaps something was slipped into her food or drink."

"Ah, Des," Nick said, one hand soothing through my hair. "Did you set your coke down at any time tonight?"

I thought about it, saw myself set it down on the bathroom sink for a moment. "In the bathroom," I answered. "It sat for a sec and I took one last sip before dumping it down the drain." Had I left my coke unattended? I couldn't remember.

Nick swore under his breath and the man said, "Miss, I'm the manager here. You may have been drugged. I'm going to call an ambulance."

"No," I said. "I'm fine now." I tilted my head to look at Nick. "Just take me home, please. I want to go home."

He cupped my cheek. "You've been drugged, hon—"

"And it's run its course," I cut in, leaning into his broad hand. I believed I'd been drugged because I needed to. Simple as that. "Please, Nick, let's go home."

Chapter 17

I made every move in agonizing slow motion...and they gained on me. I tripped on the stairs and it was no surprise, somehow, I'd known I would. They scurried up the next stair and crawled over me, thousands of them. I felt their legs and bodies on every inch of skin—under my clothes, in my hair, covering me in a black, moving blanket as they bit and pinched, filled my mouth.

I jackknifed up in bed on a loud gasp. My eyes widened, clenched shut, and my heart beat a fast drum roll in my chest and ears. Rat-a-tat-tat. Sticky from sweat, I trembled and sat panting like a dog chained out in the sun, each breath burning as it shuddered from my lungs.

After a moment, my sluggish hands crept to my face and hair checking for bugs. Miracles and wonders abounded—none was found. Flinging myself backward with an impatient huff and flipping on my side, I frowned at the bedside clock.

Just past nine. I was sorely disappointed to have missed my favorite Saturday morning cartoon—Superman. There's just something I find irresistible about a strong man in tights.

Warm and lazy minutes passed where I sprawled safe in my own bed, in my own room, in my own house, serene in the knowledge that the biggest creepy crawly thing inside its four walls was a lone spider named Charlotte. Her home is behind the downstairs toilet and neither Aunt P nor I have the heart to kill her.

Flashing my molars in a huge yawn, I rolled out of bed, stood and stretched, groaning, then scratched at the tangled mass of wild curls springing atop my head. You haven't seen bedhead until you've seen my hair in the morning. It's quite a sight. I've lost combs in it before.

Rumor has it there are people in the world who actually wake smiling. I'm not one of them. Good cheer doesn't hit me until mid-morning-ish, long after I've showered, read the paper, and liberally dosed myself with my two favorite food groups: caffeine and sugar.

I took a boiling hot shower to melt away lingering thoughts of covens and arachnids, changed into a sports bra, shorts and tee. A morning run beckoned at the tippytop of my to-do list. Squeezing in two or three jogs per week is my goal and though I always try, I often fall short of the self-imposed quota. I blame it on my job—the odd hours and all that—a handy, logical excuse. Works for me.

I turned right at the foot of the stairs and entered the dining room, which has an easterly lay with more windows than wall and on sunny mornings like that Saturday, comes alive with warm light. Above the table, the chandelier gleams and sparkles with dancing prisms along an intricate tray ceiling. Aunt P restrained herself in the room and painted it a bold, deep red. Trust me, that's mighty restrained for her, but the color fits somehow and although we seldom require the formality of the room, I often find myself in it just the same.

That morning I discovered grapes resting in a glass bowl on the sidebar. Unsuspecting, I popped one into my mouth. It tasted as green as it looked and my whole body shook and puckered with its sharp bite. My eyes complained, too, and I blinked away fat tears. To the kitchen I dashed to wash down the bitter sting. Armand sat at the table laughing softly with Aunt P and when I entered, he stood.

"*Matin,*" he said with eyes as warm and trailing as his voice.

"I hope that means there's plenty of coffee left." I grabbed a cup from the overhead cabinet. Armand held the coffeepot aloft and filled my cup. "Morning, *mon chou.*"

At his rate, I felt convinced I would have a good grasp of rudimentary French by the time he returned to Paris. And that would be soon, I was sure of it.

I mumbled a greeting back, sipped at my black, heavily sugared caffeine, and thanked him. He supplied a gracious nod as Aunt P watched avidly from the kitchen table, as if we were as mesmerizing as her afternoon soap operas. I kissed her cheek, parked myself to her left and Armand's right. The newspaper, thick with ads, lay spread over the tabletop and I rifled through the jumble for my favorite section. My face promptly buried in it—clearly discouraging conversation. Clearly. It didn't work.

Aunt P's voice held thick speculation when she broke the silence. "Why did Nick tuck you in bed last night? He hasn't done that since…hmmm, ninth grade, I believe, when Snowball ran away and you cried yourself sick."

My fingers tightened on the paper and I peered at her over its top edge, reluctant to tell either truth or lie about the previous night. Armand looked on, awaiting my response. I ignored him and hedged with Aunt P. "I thought you were asleep."

She smiled, brown eyes alight with humor, her white hair styled in short, soft curls, and countered, "Wide awake."

"Snowball?" Armand asked.

"Her cat," she answered.

"It was after eleven," I informed. *She's never up past ten,* I thought.

"Male or female?" he questioned.

I verified, "Female," and huffed when Aunt P repeated, "Wide awake."

"I'm sorry if we woke you," I said, still stalling.

She waved her hand negligently, "You didn't. Were you upset last night?"

"Snowball the cat?" Armand butted in, clearly confused.

I looked at him. "She was all white," and turned to Aunt P. "I felt a little off. It was nothing really."

"Something you ate?" Concern laced her voice.

"Possibly," I said with a shrug and dived back into the paper.

Armand asked, "Did she return?"

In stereo, my aunt and I echoed, "Who?" I eyed him over page 5E.

His lips twitched and held as much amusement as his dark eyes. "Snowball, the white cat."

"We never found her, no," Aunt P said.

"Ah, a pity. She obviously felt needed more elsewhere."

I frowned at him. "What in the world are you talking about?"

"Your familiar."

"My what?"

He tilted his head while weighing my question's sincerity. "Snowball was your familiar, your companion. She served to attend and guard you."

I snorted. "Are you nuts?"

Aunt P kicked me under the table. Thump.

I gave her a quick glare and rubbed my shin as he replied, "Witches have always had animals as their familiars. Surely you know this, *oui*? I suspect Snowball left because you didn't practice your craft."

I snorted again. "I suspect she left because she found someone to feed her table scraps instead of dirt-cheap, bargain dry food. She owned an enormous appetite."

Aunt P cackled, sounding like a cross between a hyena and a tuba, and she sipped her coffee while I shook my head at Armand. Really, I thought, he was just too much.

"Don't be surprised if a cat," he said, "a new familiar, comes to you soon." His eyes smiled at me. "Now that you're a practicing witch."

I tossed my unread paper on the table and folded my arms against my chest, the motion easy to perform with my sports bra on. "I am *not* a practicing witch."

"Desy," he admonished.

The telephone's shrill ring interrupted my cutting retort. I'm sure it would have been quite impressive, a real doozie. As a poor second, on my way to the phone I gave Armand the stink eye.

"House of horrors and mad Frenchmen," I said into the receiver.

"You're sounding chipper. Are you feeling better?"

Nick. I wondered why he'd used the house's line and not my cell.

"I'm good as gold. No need to be concerned."

"Well, I was, and when you didn't answer your cell phone this morning, I really became worried."

"You called earlier?"

"Twice," he said and I tried to remember where I'd last seen my phone.

"Oh," I breathed. "My cell's still in my jeans. Sorry."

"No problem, but if you're really feeling all right, I wondered if you'd be up to working today?"

My hand squeezed the phone. "Sarah Reynolds?" I fired, hard and quick like two bullets.

"No, the Whitcomb case."

My crushing hold eased. "You're kidding! I thought you were still wallowing in paperwork and it wouldn't start until next week."

"Me too, but they pushed everything through quicker than expected."

"Oh, okay." I frowned down at my jogging attire. "Can you send the file to me here?"

"Sure. I'm glad you're okay."

"Thanks, me too. Bye."

I turned to find an avid audience of two hanging on my every word. "I've got to go to work." Armand followed me from the room and up the stairs. Outside my bedroom, I turned to him. "Is there a particular reason you're shadowing my every move?"

"We need to talk."

I rolled my eyes. "I'm beginning to see why those four tiny words can strike terror in every man's heart." I pushed open my door. "Listen, if you want to discuss anything that begins with a 'w', for instance wizards, warlocks or witchcraft, count me out."

I made to step inside my room but he clasped my upper arm. Through narrowed eyes I looked at his hand, his face. His eyes dove into mine seeking answers I was unwilling to give.

Armand's voice lowered to an urgent whisper. "Tonight is the full moon."

I leaned toward him with my own urgent whisper. "And I don't care if the cow jumps over it either. Makes no difference to me."

Shaking off his hold, I backed into my room and took great satisfaction in closing the door in his handsome face. I searched my closet. Man, I huffed, stewing; he was like a damn dog with a bone—witches, moons, and endless discussions of the two. Hangers slid around until I found something acceptable, something that would cover the clip-on belt attachment for my Taser. I refused to wear that ankle rig again. It made a scab.

I changed and retrieved all my goodies from my jeans, transferring everything to my outfit, a form-fitting pantsuit in dove gray, an old favorite. Beneath the jacket my gun rested unnoticeable. I downloaded and printed the case, double-checked everything and declared myself ready. Ta-da!

My door opened to reveal Armand still there, pesky as a flea, leaning against the doorjamb with his hands buried in his pockets. Handsome. Elegant. Smooth. My lips firmed and I used a hand to nudge by him, touched his chest in the doing and immediately remembered what it felt like, tasted like, looked like, and trotted all the quicker down the stairs.

Grabbing my purse from the foyer closet, I pivoted to find him standing nearly on top of me. I sighed. "If I throw a stick, will you go away?"

"We need to prepare." He raked a hand through his hair, heavy frustration weighing his action and features. "There's so little time now."

I yanked open the front door. "If you're still babbling about full moons and battles, I've already told you I want no part of it."

His arms reached for me but fell to his sides in heavy resignation. "This is extremely important. Damian is readying." His face held a tortured frown. "You'll not reconsider?"

My gaze searched his features, his dark hair falling between collar and shoulder, the arch of raven brows above eyes that veered with emotion from dark chocolate to ebony. The way his nose fell strong and straight above firm lips, the lower one slightly fuller than the top, and the hint of stubbornness curving his strong jaw.

Armand made a deep sound in the back of his throat and closed the small gap between our bodies, leaned toward my mouth.

I smelled his cologne, felt his body heat, his intoxicating presence, and instinctively backed away in self-preservation. On the covered porch I said, "No, I won't reconsider," and straightened my shoulders. The words, "I'm sorry," popped out unplanned and my eyes burned. It was allergies.

A people pleaser, I'm not. No is a very active word in my vocabulary. That aside, standing on my porch that morning, looking at Armand and knowing I let him down, severely disappointed him, well, it bothered me. Stuck in my craw. The knowledge itched under my skin like a spreading rash followed by a quick chaser of anger over how he made me feel lower than an earthworm—a squirmy, dirty parasite fit only for the bottom of his shoe. "Hey," I said over a sharp smile, "there're grapes in the dining room. You should really have some. They're delish."

Jacqueline Meadows

Chapter 18

A soft contemporary is what they call them, I mused; a term coined to mollify prospective buyers who disliked the words modern and house used in the same sentence. Real estate agents dreamed up the phrase a while back and the ploy worked wonders for sales.

I sat parked down the street from Thomas Whitcomb's residence, a two-storied mishmash of stucco, angles, and windows. If it's true every house has its own personality, Thomas's said cold and stuck up—a poor first impression if you asked me.

The independent insurance firm of Cambridge Services Group offered us the Whitcomb case. They manage worker's compensation claims and proposed it as a trial in their search for a new detective agency.

Nick and I hoped to secure them as a full-time client to steady our firm's cash flow. Detective work pays in fits and starts that don't always mesh with due dates on car loans or mortgages. It's a yin and yang thing.

The case concerned suspected fraud, a straightforward insurance claim verification. Two weeks prior, brothers Thomas and Charles Whitcomb's claim forms skipped merrily into the insurance agency with three red flags waving fast and high. Flag one, new employees most often attempt health insurance scams and the brothers barely worked a month before filing. Flag two, brothers Whitcomb made their claims and took leaves of absence within days of each other. And flag three—you're out—they worked together at the same automotive stamping plant, suffered from an identical back injury. Can you say duh?

In order to tackle the case, Nick and I split the brothers — he had Charlie that day, and I, Tom. They lived within forty minutes of each other and, frankly, didn't sound like the sharpest crayons in the box to me. Bottom line? Catch Thomas Whitcomb, age 32 and single, happily up and about using his back.

In order to do that, I concluded, I needed to somehow mosey into his backyard. Why? Well, because that's where all the fun was happening. Mr. Whitcomb's driveway buzzed with activity that sunny Saturday morning. New landscaping, by the look of it, all being hauled behind the house. Numerous perennials in one-gallon containers, several saplings and bushes wrapped in burlap, along with a huge mountain of shredded cedar mulch, graced his drive.

If you were paying through the nose for landscaping and currently on leave from work, where would you be? For Tommy Whitcomb, I bet the backyard.

Trucks from Sherwood Forest Nursery and Landscaping were aligned single file along the curb. The nursery is one that I'm quite familiar with. They have half a dozen landscape designers on staff at each of their six locations. Tons of employees, certainly not a mom and pop organization.

I seriously doubted if any of the hardworking landscape menials I witnessed using shovels and wheelbarrows would know me from Adam. Just the pretense I needed to take a gander at the backyard and hopefully, Mr. Whitcomb in the flesh, bending.

In preparation, I undid the top two buttons of my suit, exposing a healthy amount of cleavage (tacky but effective) and turned on my work purse, hard-wired with a video camera, built-in antenna and full audio. The overall lens size is as tiny as a coin. Does the job, though, and beautifully. If Tommy was being a bad boy, it'd catch him in 105,000 full-color pixels.

I sauntered up the drive and headed straight for the closest male, a short, sweaty specimen in cutoffs and work boots. I greeted him and he paused in loading hostas into the wheelbarrow, swiped a forearm across his wet brow and squinted at me. "I'm the designer for this job. Is Mr. Whitcomb around?" I asked.

"The customer? Yeah." He owned a heavy smoker's voice so hoarse I had a quick mental image of his lungs as two black balloons. He jacked his thumb up and tipped it towards the rear yard. "Back there."

"Thanks." I headed for the sounds of shovels digging, men's voices and the familiar, pleasant aroma of dirt.

I'd studied a small photo of Whitcomb in my Jeep—just a headshot used on his work ID card, so I searched the masculine faces and approached Mr. Whitcomb's profile.

He stood near the landscapers with hands on his hips, arguing about the placement of peony bushes. I quietly sidled alongside him and stood unnoticed for a few seconds, taking good advantage of the time to look him over.

Tall, that's the word to describe him, maybe standing six-foot-five or six. And butt ugly. Aunt P would say that Thomas Whitcomb must have fallen from an ugly tree and hit every branch on his way down. His facial features were askew, as if after his fall they were reassembled incorrectly with a few pieces shoved willy nilly where they obviously didn't belong. Brownish hair, cropped military short, sprouted like whiskers on his head and his nose peaked off-center, sitting short and squat between beady eyes of watery blue. His otherwise slim frame sported a potbelly; the tight roundness rolled over his plaid shorts as a clear testament to his penchant for fermented hops and barley.

A snazzy dresser, Tommy, modeling a wrinkled tee shirt of over-washed, dull black, spotted indiscriminately with stains of unknown origin above shorts one size too small, and untied dirty, grayish sneakers encasing his feet. He looked ready to grace the hallowed pages of GQ.

Overall impression? Just a poor schmuck whose spare time probably involved an inflatable doll or two. I interrupted his whining.

"...and I'm tellin' ya, those flowers should go in deeper," he said.

"Actually," I said, "they shouldn't go there at all."

Tommy's head swiveled and looked down at me from the heavens. "And you'd be?"

"Hi, I'm the landscape designer." I held out my hand. "Maria Milcott." (I pluck names randomly from my imagination. That day it was Maria, the next it might very well be Samantha Salamander.) I purposely omitted the name of Sherwood Forest in my introduction to steer clear of misrepresentation. However you cut the mustard, alluding would land me in much less trouble. The worker closest to us used the distraction to take his shovel and slink away. I couldn't blame him.

Whitcomb eyed my hand before briefly clasping it, like I had communicable girly germs, scratched behind his ear, and sniffed sinuses gurgling full and phlegmy. Poor baby had a cold or allergies, I thought, or perhaps both. I smiled.

"Ain't hired no designer," he objected.

"Oh, we have a drawing once a week and the lucky customer receives design services with their purchase, free of charge."

"Free?"

"Yes, and those peonies," I said, pointing, "are full sun plants. You'll have to move them a few feet from the maple tree." I glanced around his yard. "Near your deck would be ideal." Facing him, I bent to pick up a bush and fumbled with it, adding a few grunts for good measure before tilting my face to him. "These are just so heavy!" I resisted batting my eyelashes.

A smirk worked at his mouth, part leer at my bent position and the free show of Wonderbra cleavage. He hitched his droopy shorts and lifted the peony. I smiled my appreciation of his manly strength.

Men are so easy. Well, some of them anyway. Mr. Whitcomb, certainly. I stayed for a couple hours that morning directing him and the nursery staff around the yard in a landscape plan of my own design. I think it turned out quite nice. And all the while my trusty camera whirred away while Tommy I've-injured-my-back-and-can-barely-walk Whitcomb lifted and hauled to impress me.

Evidently he took to me because he asked for my home phone number before I left. I smoothed on what I could only assume was a becoming, grateful smile and gave Mr. Whitcomb the number to Great Lakes Funeral Home.

Chapter 19

It looked ordinary…and empty, certainly not the setting of the most surreal, frightening memory I owned (up to that point). There was more fun to come before week's end but I was, of course, unaware.

My takeout lunch of a boxed salad and diet Coke sat untouched on the passenger seat as I peered through my windshield at Club Wicked's vacant parking lot. Outside the front entrance, nothing stirred. Not one car. Not one person.

I could've rationalized that I just happened in the neighborhood and ended up at the club by happenstance rather than design, but why lie to myself? My Jeep battled twenty minutes through weekend traffic crawling with carloads of busy people on errands and shopping expeditions to get there…on purpose.

Daytime leached life from the building. It stood alone and somber in the sunshine, looming out of place, expressionless, looking no more able to house a secret coven than the Wendy's down the road. I supposed the bright lights, pounding music and hundreds of patrons brought it alive each night. An empty shell, that's all it really was. Innocent.

I settled back in my seat and sighed, having driven there for answers, some type of confirmation. I wanted the club to shout evil and guilt, wanted it to say Yes, Desy, what you experienced the previous night was real, not some drug-induced vision. Instead, it said nothing. Solitary and voiceless, that's what it was, four walls of steel and brick disappointment.

Why would a girl spike my drink in the john? I wondered. Why would I hallucinate of witches and beetles of all things while hallucinatory monkey sex with Brad Pitt would have been much more pleasant? Why did I believe I saw Sarah Reynolds the previous night? Why did these questions keep circling my brain like fast, dangerous cars at a racetrack? Sooner or later one or more of them would crash and break apart. Then I'd have peace.

I sighed again and eyed my lunch. The jury was still out on my appetite. I didn't seem to have much of one so far that day.

The ringing of my cell phone cut short another sigh of frustration. The ID read Nick's home number. "Hey handsome, wassup dawg?"

"Where's Nick?" My spine straightened at the snapping voice. It was Anita, his sweet, loving wife. Notice there was no, "Hello Desy, how are you doing? Beautiful day, isn't it?" For some reason, we really *did not* get along. No siree. We were like two cats meeting in a back alley. Each encounter held lots of hissing and hair-raising fun along with the sure knowledge only one kitty would strut away intact. Thankfully, we seldom ran into each other, much less conversed.

I used my best saccharin sweet voice, thick as honey dripping from a hive. "Is this Anita?"

"You know full well it is," she snapped. "Where's my husband? Is he meeting you for lunch?"

"Gee," I mused, "I'm not sure where Nicky's at. Did you try his cell?"

"Of course I did," she shot in her you're-as-stupid-as-a-brick icy tone. "He's not answering."

"Afraid I can't help you then."

"You know where he's at, don't you?"

I sighed into the phone, seemingly just chockfull of extra breath that day. Did that mean I was full of hot air? "If he's not answering, he's probably still on the case."

"Which case?"

"You know I can't divulge that."

"Bullshit! I need to speak with him, Desdemona. Now." She always pronounces my name like a curse word. Spits it at me, all obscene and vile, like a putdown. It never hits the mark, though, as I quite like my name…well, my first one anyway.

"Is this an emergency? Because if your house isn't being ransacked or you're not bleeding profusely, you'll just have to wait until he turns his cell back on."

She gave a little shriek in my ear and hung up. I set down my phone, smiled, and reached for my salad.

My appetite had returned.

* * * * *

He was gorgeous, the drop dead kind. I'd just spent a couple hours around half-naked, sweaty men and hadn't felt a thing, not even a twinge. But this one, well, he had flurries of excitement dancing the merengue in my stomach, and I didn't like it. Not one bit.

I came home to an empty house and a small note in Aunt P's illegible scrawl propped on the kitchen table. As near as I made out, she was either in the backyard next to the vegetable garden…or in northern Peru smoking handmade cigars with Bigfoot.

Squinting at the note, I bet on the former and changed into shorts and a tee shirt before slipping on my green gardening clogs. She sat in the shade of the patio umbrella with a shirtless Armand digging nearby in my garden. Surprise flashed through me. I hadn't figured Mr.-Tailored-Clothes-Three-Piece-Armani-Suit-Guy capable of getting dirty.

Shining in the sun, his hair fell in a rich curtain of deep, dark chocolate, swinging with each push of the shovel through soil. Muscles bunched in his arms, legs and torso as he worked, and khakis covered his hips. Barely.

From years of training and exercise, Chen was built stronger, but Armand's body was no less mouth-watering. He has a presence to him. Manly Hunk, it says. When I realized I stood comparing the two men, I winced and headed for my aunt.

"Hi." I kissed her cheek. She patted my shoulder and I plopped beside her.

That day Aunt P dressed conservatively in a fluorescent orange housedress bright enough to force a squint. On her head perched a straw hat; a wide purple ribbon graced its band and dancing merry on its rim were yellow plastic flowers.

"Have you had lunch?" she asked.

I heard the shovel stop working in the dirt behind me and did my best not to turn around. "Yep." A pitcher sat sweating on the patio table. "Your famous lemonade?"

She nodded. "Would you like some?"

"Yes indeedy-do." And I stood to pour but found only two glasses. "Oh." She'd left the note for me in the kitchen but obviously hadn't really expected me back so soon.

"I'll just go in and grab another glass, sweetie pie," she offered.

Armand's voice trailed over my shoulder. "There's no need, Desy and I will share." He moved behind me and pulled his chair so close to mine a thin hair couldn't fit between. He sat wearing a smile, some sweat, and not much else. I pretended he affected me not the slightest, pictured him as a half-witted smelly sumo wrestler with a lisp, and nonchalantly poured the drinks—one for Aunt P and one for Yokomisha and myself to share.

I set the glass in front of him. "Here, you first." I sat.

He held it aloft. "*Mon chou*, ladies first."

"Fine." I snatched the glass and gulped three long swallows. He studied me as I drank and his gaze lowered to my mouth. Humor shone in his eyes and something else as well. Heat. I almost choked.

I found myself licking my lips, holding his gaze while passing him the lemonade. His fingers brushed mine and he turned the glass to where I'd left a faint trace of red lipstick. I wear the kind that promises to set firm and not wear off. They lie. Whatever happened to truth in advertising? Or is that now an oxymoron along with no-run pantyhose and honest politicians?

Anyway, Armand drank and I watched his throat work as the liquid slid down. A breath I hadn't known I held released when Aunt P's snicker floated through the air. I ignored the message in her twinkling eyes. "So, you put Armand to work preparing the garden. Are we still going with the new tomatoes?"

Every winter Aunt P and I plot our summer vegetable garden on paper. We discuss and plan and compromise our way through countless seed catalogs. She keeps pushing to widen the garden area but since I perform the hard labor, I keep pushing back. Through our houseguest, I suspected she'd discovered a way to worm around my resistance.

I cast a glance at Armand. Shouldn't have. He smiled and pressed his leg against mine. Hairs brushed and tickled my calf.

"Yes," my aunt said.

"Yes what?" I asked.

"The tomatoes, dear."

Heat burned up my neck. "Oh, sorry...I was...daydreaming."

Her lips curved and Armand inquired, "About?"

I refused to look at him and mumbled, "Something inconsequential," before taking another drink of our lemonade. Snaking around the back of my chair, his fingers toyed gently in my hair. I tensed and leaned forward a margin. His fingers followed. "I didn't picture you as the outdoorsy-type, Armand."

"All witches are drawn to nature," he told me. "Our craft is the art and science of living in balance with the environment and one's will."

"Yeah?" I said. "Well in that case, can I *will* the garden to plant itself this year?"

He gave my hair a gentle tug. "*Mon chou*, what would be the fun in that?"

My aunt commented, "I was thinking of adding cucumbers this year."

"That sounds nice but we'd have to get rid of beans or lettuce to make room." Armand pulled lightly on one long curl, skimming his fingertips against my nape. Chill bumps broke along my heated skin.

"Well, Armand has offered to widen the garden this year for us," Aunt P said. "Isn't that wonderful?"

"Mmm, wonderful," I murmured, completely distracted. For all I knew, we were discussing taxidermy.

Aunt P smiled over her easy victory and thanked Armand.

"It's my pleasure," he assured. Part melt-in-your-mouth sexiness, part arrogance waxed his smooth tone. Both parts raised my blood pressure.

Pretending he was a foul-smelling sumo wrestler just wasn't working. Each breeze carried his scent and it was anything but foul. A battle of wills, that's what it felt like to me. He could rub his leg along mine and fiddle with my hair all day long. I would rise to the challenge by showing him, and my crafty aunt, absolutely no response. No reaction. Not one. Nada. He wasn't going to unsettle me and that was that! If he thought otherwise, well, he was—"Stop!" I hissed.

His fingers stilled. "*Excusez-moi*." I made the mistake of looking at him, his face leaning so close to mine, and felt such an intoxicating wave of heat, I stood abruptly. He followed suit.

"I've got housework to do," I said, and fumbled with my chair, pushing it back. "Clothes to wash and…um, more clothes to wash." I couldn't leave the backyard quick enough.

"Oh, I hoped we could discuss the garden more," Aunt P stalled. Her eyes held glee and a shiny twinkle.

"Sorry, a week's worth of dirty laundry is calling my name." Under normal circumstances, I'd have loved to sit with my aunt and talk gardening, dirty clothes be damned. But that wasn't a normal circumstance; it was cruel and unusual punishment. I had to leave, right that very minute.

As I circled behind Armand, he captured my hand and raised it to his mouth. Instead of kissing my knuckles, his lips pressed hot against my palm and I nearly jumped out of my clogs when he flicked his tongue. Snatching back my hand quicker than if I'd been scalded, I marched away.

Chapter 20

With the swish and whir of the washer and dryer droning in the background, and only dirty clothes for company, I stood in the basement mulling over the Reynolds case while I sorted laundry.

Nick and I had exhausted every lead. I broke down and even read Sarah's diary in the hope he missed something. He hadn't, of course. Nick's sharp.

Half an hour earlier, I tried his cell but it was still turned off. After text messaging him an update on my part of the Whitcomb case and entering my notes into the upstairs computer, I reviewed Sarah's file again for the umpteenth time. Ignoring the incident at the club, standard procedure in a case like hers was to widen the search. We'd already spoken with her friends, classmates, parents and thoroughly searched her car, bedroom and hangouts. It was time to check back with the police and investigate further any connection to the other missing teens from bordering school districts.

However, ignoring the incident at the club became harder and harder to do. For my own benefit, if not Sarah's, there was no getting around the fact I needed to return there—and not under the sun's safe rays, but at night during normal business hours.

Deep in thought, I hefted a full clothesbasket and climbed the stairs. I would grab the manager of Club Wicked and persuade him to allow me access to the VIP room. A few planted phrases of 'spiked drink' and 'possible lawsuit' would be an excellent inducement.

I walked distracted into the hallway and turned to climb the second set of stairs to my room. Aunt P progressed down them and paused midway. "Oh, good," she said. "I was just coming down to find you. Armand has invited us to dinner this evening."

She smiled and took her next step but the placement of her foot fell wrong. My blood froze while the very air in my lungs seized and twisted hard as I watched the beginning seconds of her stumble. She stood several steps up, too far for me to reach in time, but I tried anyway. The clothesbasket dropped and my arms reached out as I sprinted upward. I yelled, "No—Stop!"

In a panic you blurt the strangest things. Like when a man wielding a knife charges someone and they say, "Don't hurt me!" As if that would really help. Or like ordering No and Stop as if mere words could actually prevent a fall.

Somehow though, miraculously, they did.

The world stopped. Well, my small part of it anyway. Aunt P stood frozen in time, locked in a macabre position on the stairs with one leg ready to collapse and her entire body caught in a forward falling motion.

An erratic noise roared in my ears and I realized it was my own heartbeat. With hesitant steps I climbed the remaining stairs. Still, she was so very still, and my hand curved tentatively around her slim shoulder. There was no movement, no acknowledgement, no breath, not even one blink from her. Air whooshed from my lungs and I nearly toppled down the stairs myself in my frantic downward scramble.

I stood on shaky legs at the foot of the stairs staring at my aunt, my hand trembling over my mouth. Her dear face held surprised shock. She knew she was going to fall; the knowledge screamed in her eyes. She clutched the banister—her fingers curved there still—but even had she managed to hold on during her topple, she wouldn't save her ankle. It curved in an awkward position centimeters from snapping on the next step.

I'd stopped her. Knew it without doubt. Frozen her in place like a living ice sculpture. It'd been me. How long would she stay like that? I wondered. One second longer? Forever?

Armand, my mind whispered. I needed Armand. I sprinted from the room shouting his name, flying past clocks whose hands were frozen, past the kitchen's small television set with its picture stilled on a silent commercial, into the yard.

He saw my mad sprint and his welcoming smile transformed to concerned frown. I bulldozed right into him. The shovel fell as he grabbed my upper arms and he stumbled three steps before regaining his balance.

"What is it?" His eyes narrowed and he shook me. "You're as white as a sheet. What's wrong?" A bead of sweat rolled slowly down his temple, disappearing into his sideburn, and I found myself staring at his ear. It was a nice ear. The next second he squeezed my arms and pulled me upright. "*Non*, don't you faint on me." He shook me again and kissed me hard, nudging aside my shock.

"Aunt P!" I wheezed. "Going to fall—I—she's—frozen."

"*Merde*," he breathed. "Come."

We ran inside and stood at the foot of the stairs looking up. I clutched him like a frightened child who'd heard a noise at bedtime.

"It takes many months, sometimes years, to master this particular power." He stroked my hair. "I am still unable to perform it."

"How long will she stay like that?" I asked in a reedy whisper.

"You shouldn't have been able to do this in the first place. I could only speculate."

"I'll take a speculation please."

After a quick shrug of his shoulders he said, "Anywhere from a few minutes to a few hours—certainly not overnight." I made a strangled sound and Armand curved his body around mine. "You can undo this. You must master your powers and learn how to revoke spells as well as weave them." He pressed his face against mine and spoke softly in my ear. "Come, I'll help you."

I sucked in one calming breath before he pulled me up the stairs. He stood in my aunt's path, positioned me down and over a step. "What is the word you used?"

I tore my gaze from Aunt P's frozen form and met his eyes. "I said no, stop."

He braced himself to steady her. "To rescind your spell, concentrate on her and say the opposite."

My brow furrowed in disbelief. It couldn't be that simple. "What — like yes and go?"

The air wavered instantaneously, shimmered alive, and my aunt moved, following through on her fall, as if I first hit a pause button, then the one marked play. But instead of tripping down the stairs and breaking there, she stumbled into Armand's waiting arms. He grunted.

"Good gravy!" she gasped. "I didn't even see you, Armand. Forgive me." She pushed from him slightly and patted his shoulder. "Are you all right dear?"

He smiled and held her firm. "*Oui*, think nothing of it. The question is, are you unhurt?"

"Yes, I believe so."

"Let's see, shall we?" He assisted her downstairs. "Your right ankle, it's well?"

Aunt P peered down. "It feels the tiniest bit sore." Wiggling it with ease, she looked at him and smiled. "It'll be fine," then scolded me with, "Well don't just stand there, Desy my girl, you've dropped your basket of clothes all over the floor here. Someone could trip and fall." Armand flashed me a quick grin before escorting her from the foyer.

My legs gave and I slumped like a rag doll to perch limp on the stair. It was all I could manage.

Chapter 21

Armand found me ten minutes later. My mind replayed in sickening detail Aunt P's near fall—the shock on her face at that moment, and on mine, but instead of ending it there, it filled in the 'what if' scenario. What if I hadn't stopped her and she'd continued her flight down the stairs?

I was an unwilling audience as my mind's eye displayed in crisp color images Aunt P's bouncing fall to the bottom of the stairs. It panned to her broken body lying still, twisted oddly, bent, and me standing over her, scared and useless. My own private horror-show, free of charge.

Fingers softly stroked my cheek, the skin wet. The caress felt abstract, distant, as if petting me through a thick winter coat.

Endearments feathered in warm whispers against my ear, some in English, some not, and the room swayed as strong arms carried me into the living room and arranged me on a masculine lap.

I sat for ten minutes or ten hours or ten days. Two broad hands stroked me without pause, one massaging my thigh, the other rubbing my back, and words were spoken. Soft words, coaxing words, persuasive words. I fought my way through thick fog and focused.

"*Bebe*, tell me you're all right. Snap at me. Fight with me. Argue. I need to hear your voice."

"What you *need* is a shower," I whispered to Armand. "You're all sticky." I leaned into him even more, pressing closer against his warm, solid flesh.

He chuckled and said in an intimate voice, "That's my girl, welcome back. How do you feel?"

My stomach wrenched sour as I thought of my aunt. "Aunt P!" I started to push from him but he held firm.

"Shhh, Penelope's fine. She's resting in the sunroom. I made her a cup of tea."

"Her ankle?"

"Is fine as well, *mon chou*."

"God," I breathed and circled my arms around his neck, hugging tight, burying my face into the smooth hollow. A pulse throbbed there, strong and sure, and I counted its beat: one-thousand-one, one-thousand-two, one-thousand-three. Scents registered — tangy sweat, faint cologne, and Armand.

I grappled with my thoughts. "I've read books on magic, on witchcraft. Nowhere did I read that time could be…frozen with just a word or two. Spells are cast with forethought. They're planned out. You need candles and…and crystals, things you showed me in my bedroom that day. I don't understand." I sighed. "I thought if I didn't ever mumble rhyming verses or line up rocks in a nice tidy circle, magic would leave me alone. I even threw away all my candles."

"Is being a witch so terrible you would do such a thing?" He stilled beneath me and his chest expanded with trapped air, baited breath.

"If you had asked me that just this morning, I'd've said yes. But my aunt's safe and unhurt because of magic, my magic, and now I'm just not so sure anymore."

Armand exhaled softly. His hand trailed up my back and delved into my hair, playing in my curls while he explained. "You and I are different, highborn, if you will. The magic you read about doesn't pertain to High Priests and Priestesses. We are far beyond most practicing witches. We're of a different class."

"Why now?" I asked, pushing from his chest. "I've lived all my life without this…this magic." My hand sliced the air. "It's like a switch has been thrown inside me. Why?"

Armand framed my face. "Because now you believe."

A peevish note floated within me, surfacing in my consciousness, bobbing hard and small and shiny, whispering I wouldn't have 'believed' without his influence. If he hadn't come to town, I would've been fine and dandy. I no more believed in witchcraft a week ago than in little green men from Mars. It was all his fault.

He must have seen something hard flash in my eyes because he used a low voice to caution, "Desy." He dipped his head, angling his mouth toward mine. I pulled back at once and felt a blockage in my throat, a kind of tense pressure. His face stilled and the moment stretched taut between us as his eyes searched mine, scorching in their quest.

Still cradling my face, he spoke in a voice of soft velvet. "Let me." His lips neared. "Let me, *mon chou*." Could I have refused? Broken loose? Yes and yes. I could have and very probably would have had I possessed functioning gray matter and one thought that wasn't of him.

My eyes closed instead.

We kissed.

Armand moaned low and hungry and eager against my mouth just before slipping his tongue inside. Blame it on shock, perhaps, but I went absent, thoroughly lost, and not looking to be found. Nothing else mattered or even existed—just his mouth, his tongue, his scent, and the heady sensations ripping through me.

Along my lips and jawline he nibbled using teasing bites, small nips, hot and restless, while excited tingles of pleasure bolted through me. Armand's hands grasped my hips and he feathered warm coaxing whispers against my ear. "Come closer," he said. "Sit astride me. Come, I'll help you." Eager to obey, I straddled him.

Armand murmured his pleasure in English spattered with French and I dipped my head to lick his nipple, feeling it tighten into a smooth brown nub. He shuddered and voiced a low, rumbling hum, almost a purr of appreciation, and I couldn't help smiling against his smooth skin, crisp hair, before moving my mouth across his chest.

"Closer," he urged. His hands filled with the curves of my ass, plumping them in a flexing hold. "I need you closer." He eased me forward and beneath me his cock bulged, its hard length pressing thick and ready between my legs. I remembered what it looked like, felt like in my hands, tasted like in my mouth, and with the memory I trembled.

I raised my face to find his gaze burning a fiery black, swirling with passion, and as my hands slid into his hair, my lips met his. He moaned again and the needy vibration sent a quiver prancing up and down my spine. Our tongues tangled wet and languid with enough heat to ignite wet wood.

Armand rocked his hips, rotating in a sensuous orbit, the maddening motion rubbing his cock against me, and his hand stole to the front of my thigh. Near the hem his fingers loitered, circling under my shorts, before creeping between my spread legs.

Blunt fingertips teased in lazy circles against the wet crotch of my panties, raking there lightly, and our kiss deepened, turned wild — tongue sliding against tongue — when he eased the sodden lace and elastic aside. He stroked me, back and forth, and again, probing along drenched hairs, plump folds, before sliding one finger up inside. I shuddered, moaned when a second finger slipped in deep. They moved together in my juices, coaxing squishy sounds to join the soft mewls I pushed into his mouth.

Armand's thumb eased over my clitoris. Again I shuddered, and my hips began to rotate with each circle of his thumb, until I thought I'd go mad with the overwhelming feel of him. Long mind-numbing minutes passed of dancing tongues, hands stroking hair, churning pelvises, and fingers sliding in and out of slick arousal. Heat suffused me and pressure climbed so fast, wound so tight; there wasn't enough air. I couldn't breathe. My mouth slipped off his to pant near his ear. "Armand," I whispered.

My splayed fingers stilled in his hair, my hips quieted, and I quivered as everything pulled tight, prickling with the fiery onrush of release. Another wave of tingly heat hit me, breaking in a hard climax against Armand's hand.

He groaned my name in a harsh whisper.

My breathing slowed, and following a soft kiss I pressed on his neck, he eased his fingers from me. I leaned back, met his burning gaze, drowned in its heat, intense and searing, then watched his fingers slip deep within his mouth. One by one he licked them clean. Armand savored my arousal for long moments, watching me watch him, before he eased me down for another kiss.

His right hand smoothed along my spine under my tee and unclasped my bra. That single action cleared my brain and opened a mental door—allowing several unwelcome thoughts to swagger inside and make themselves known—the most disturbing of which is he had unfastened the three small hooks *so damn easily*. The very casualness of it slapped...and the resounding sting said he'd likely had more women than Bond, James Bond. Where would I fall—at number 178 between the stewardess and the aerobics instructor?

The foyer clock, a massive grandfather version standing six-feet-tall, bonged five o'clock. I had a date that night. Chen and his new motorcycle were scheduled to arrive at six...look how I spent my spare time.

I stopped the kiss and hopped off his lap, very proud of the fact I stood unaided. No small accomplishment, that. I reached behind to rehook my bra when Armand said my name. Admittedly his voice always sounds incredibly sexy, but my name then on his lips sounded downright decadent, as sensual as his touch. I quivered.

"Desy," he repeated with mild force. "What's wrong?"

He looked gorgeous and rumpled; I sighed in equal parts regret and relief. I often felt way in over my head with him—completely out of my depth—as if swimming into deeper water than I expected, discovering rapids, and realizing my life preserver leaked. "I'm sorry," I said and huffed in exasperation when I fumbled at my bra's clasps. My fingers wouldn't work.

Armand stood and turned me around. Raising my shirt, he rehooked my bra and I made to step away, get some needed distance, but he wound his arms around my waist from behind. "*Non*, talk to me." He rested his chin on my shoulder, pressed his cheek against mine, and waited.

My heart sped with his thick length wedged like hot steel in the small of my back and his fingers tracing slow, mesmerizing circles on my belly. I feared internal combustion and pondered how my remains, evidenced by a neat pile of ash on the living room floor, would be explained to the firemen.

It didn't help that my overactive imagination conjured vivid images of Armand peeling down my shorts and panties in a slow tease before bending me over to plunge deep from behind. His cock would plow between my legs, shove high, and feel enormous as it drove back and forth. His pelvis would bump and slap against my ass. My rising cries would mingle with his harsh panting, and wet rhythmic sounds of slick suctioning would overfill the room. A masculine groan would rumble. Then two. And his cock would buck and spray hot seed; I would brim with cream.

God. I shuddered, held myself very still, trying not to sputter my answer. "I...I need to get ready...for dinner."

"The reservation is not for two more hours."

"What reservation?"

"I assumed Penelope told you. I'm taking you both to dinner this evening."

I recalled hearing that from Aunt P, yes I did, but I believed it was just before I zapped her with my cosmic freeze ray. I couldn't be blamed for forgetting the invitation in the ensuing fevered excitement.

I cleared my throat to swallow an apology. He'd received an awful lot of them from me and I wasn't sure he deserved yet another one. "I have a previous engagement."

His fingers stilled. "A previous engagement?"

"Yes...I have a date."

"A date."

"What's with the echo?"

"May I ask with whom?"

"You may."

He waited, sighed. Warm breath feathered past the corner of my mouth. "Whom is your date with tonight?"

"My boyfriend."

He released me and eased away. I felt so alone, bereft, I hugged myself. "Chen?" he asked.

I faced away from him and was gladdened by the fact; the note creeping into his voice told me I probably didn't want to turn around. "Yes, Chen."

Heavy rubber soles paced on hardwood floor, step-step-pivot, step-step-pivot, before moving in the direction of the couch. I heard Armand sit.

"I find it interesting you refer to him as your boyfriend, and not your lover...a favor, please," he said.

A favor? I thought. Join him again on the couch? Break my date? Polish his shoes? I breathed deep and studied the far wall where Aunt P displayed two converse prints, one a soft botanical featuring a blue hydrangea, the other a bold modern piece in reds and yellows. "Yes?"

"Ask yourself if you could do what you did with me, feel what you felt, and still call him your boyfriend."

My chin lifted of its own accord and I silently left the room, but not before I heard him softly wish me a pleasant evening.

Chapter 22

I'd never done it before and the sensation thrilled me no end, like flying in a convertible plane or perhaps riding a horse that didn't clomp, trot or neigh. "This is great!"

"I'm glad you like it but there's no need to shout. Your helmet has a headset."

I laughed. "Oh, sorry."

My hands clutching his waist, Chen flew his bike down a back road taking me to what he termed a surprise. The wind whipped, the engine roared, and the cycle vibrated as we sped past houses nestled far off the road, tree after tree after tree, and to the left, the rolling greens of a private golf course.

Heading west, Chen steered off the paved road onto a nearly hidden dirt path, advancing along a curving incline shrouded by the long hanging arms of oaks and the thick fringe of willows. I clutched him tighter and thrilled to the bumpy winding ride, the feeling of freedom.

"Almost there," he said.

I smiled my response, realized he couldn't see me and laughed at myself again. He'd managed to do for me what I had been unable to accomplish on my own: carve out a little time and put work and vexing caseloads, Aunt P and frozen staircases, Armand and irksome questions aside. Chen helped me escape.

At the ridge's top we stowed our helmets and walked hand-in-hand toward its peak. I hadn't realized how steep the cliff rose until a smiling Chen led me to its edge.

The view was beautiful. Vegetation grew all along the banks, various bushes and trees were abloom in reds, purples and soft whites, and in the valley a small stream bubbled. It looked like a postcard.

Chen squeezed my hand. "Back in a sec."

I stood spellbound while my lungs filled with fresh air and released my last bit of tension on a slow exhale. The only sounds were birdsong and moving water. Nature's ceiling blazed in bold azure and one lone, puffy cloud paused suspended like a cotton ball.

Turning to thank him, I watched delighted as he dug in a backpack and emptied its contents one by one onto a waiting blanket. "A picnic!" I cheeped with a huge grin.

Chen looked up, smiling at my expression. "You're easy," he teased. "I get a bigger smile serving dinner on the ground than I did taking you to that five-star restaurant."

I sat beside him and helped empty the pack. "Hey, it wasn't my fault that our snotty waiter had a wart on his nose the size of a small house. I couldn't stop staring at it." I mock shivered. "Put my whole dinner off, I tell you."

Chen said, "He wasn't snotty until you slipped and ordered a *wart* instead of water." We looked at each other and busted into laughter. "When you realized what you'd said, your face turned redder than their lobster special!"

"I know—and you were a *real* big help," I reproached. "Your shoulders shook so hard I thought you were having a seizure, and you hid behind your menu for an eternity!"

"I was being a gentlemen and trying to save you further embarrassment."

I shook my head. "Gentlemen don't snort behind their wine lists."

"You heard that? I thought I muffled it."

We grinned at each other and he handed me a paper plate. "I thought about packing the real stuff," he apologized, "but it might not've made it here in one piece."

"Are you kidding? Cold fried chicken always tastes better off paper," I assured. "It's in the picnic etiquette book under the chapter Ants Are Your Friends."

He kissed me. It didn't set me on fire, no, but I found solace in his arms.

✻ ✻ ✻ ✻ ✻

We walked a long, winding trail after dinner and made it back to the blanket in time to watch the setting sun. I sat in the vee of Chen's legs, leaning against his chest while his arms wrapped around my waist and his chin rested comfortably on my shoulder. I tried not to think of another man using just that same pose hours past, tried not to compare how I felt in his arms with how I felt in Chen's.

Despite a high temperature that day in the low eighties, the early evening breeze held a decided nip. That's Michigan for you. It's probably the only state that can offer both spring sledding and water skiing in the same week. We put on our jackets and wrapped the blanket around us as we talked.

"Whatever happened with your dad's car? The last I heard, it'd been towed to a repair shop."

His answer feathered soft against my neck. "Faulty gas gauge. It read half full but the tank was empty."

"Under warranty?" I asked.

"Yeah." He nuzzled my throat. "Still working on that adultery case?"

"Nope, that's been signed, sealed and delivered." I took a breath. "My latest is a missing teenage witch."

He produced a half-snort, half-chuckle. "A witch?"

A few days ago, my reaction to that word had been far more disdainful; still, it hurt to hear Chen's scorn. "Yeah, she believes in witchcraft," I said. "What do you think about witches...and magic?" I knew what he would say—what most people would say. Guess I needed to hear the words.

145

"They don't exist. And people who believe they do are—I don't know—pagan is the word I guess I'm looking for. Devil-worshippers. Over the deep end." Each word he said slapped like a personal rejection. I couldn't speak and after a moment's pause, he asked, "Have you thought over my question, Desy?"

I didn't pretend to misunderstand. He wanted to know my decision regarding commitment. Before Armand and witchcraft entered my life, the decision would have been uncomplicated. A comfortable relationship with a nice handsome man, many women would be happy with such a thing. I know—I used to be one of them.

"Desy?" he asked.

I squirmed, turned around in his arms and demanded, "Kiss me."

His lips met mine and I put my all into the kiss, concentrated hard, willed myself to feel passion and desire. He moaned, shuddered. Affection, pleasant comfort, that's all I felt, and ending the kiss, I hugged him hard.

Chen deserved a woman he could rouse more than a lukewarm response in. I had only to find the courage to tell him.

"Wow, I think…" he said, but paused to look up. A fat raindrop spattered on my head. "That it's starting to rain."

That one lone cloud I'd seen earlier made several friends and they let loose. Chen and I surged up laughing, wrestled with the blanket, and dashed to the motorcycle. By the time we stowed the cover and shoved on our helmets, we were drenched. By the time we reached my house, we were two soggy puddles. I was so wet and saturated and dripping, I felt as if I'd taken a long bath. In my clothes. In ice.

I declined Chen's invitation to his loft. A warm shower at his place, sitting around alone with him, dressed perhaps in one of his robes while my clothes tumbled dry, well, it didn't take a rocket scientist to figure where that led.

I considered reciprocating and inviting Chen inside with me to wait out the storm. I thought about sitting with him on the couch with Armand's knowing gaze weighing us from across the room and Aunt P's hair in shocking pink curlers, arms outstretched offering macaroons, and thought better.

In my driveway Chen turned off the ignition and I half-hopped, half-slid off the wet leather seat. He stowed my helmet before lifting off his own. We smiled as the rain pelted us and except for the chill, I felt in no great hurry to get inside. Wet was wet. I couldn't be more so.

Around a crooked grin I said, "I had a great time."

His smile broadened. "Despite the shower?"

"Well, you *did* promise me a surprise."

Thunder barked close and Chin kissed my forehead, my lips. "Better get inside. I'll call you."

I smiled with a wave before darting off.

Chapter 23

My home's interior was lit and warm and empty. I'd returned a smidgen past nine that night so my mind jumped to the reasonable assumption that Armand and Aunt P were still out enjoying dinner. I wished them well as I took the stairs by twos (no small accomplishment at my height) and filled the bathtub with water hot enough to poach an egg. The only man who'd seen me naked in the past year, Mr. Bubbles, sat smiling at me and I liberally sprinkled him into the tub.

A few choice words rent the air during a manic argument with my wet clothes. I won the fight by finally peeling them off in hard yanks and flinging them onto the bathroom's tiled floor. They piled in a tangled, sodden heap and I kicked them for good measure. There, take that!

I sank beneath a steaming blanket of bubbles. Groaned. Moaned. Closed my eyes and thought glory be and hallelujah.

Before I became too comfortable, though, a muffled chime hummed and I opened one exasperated eye. My pants were ringing. The water splashed on a high rolling wave when I reached over the tub's porcelain edge and dug out my cell phone. The ID proclaimed one Nicholas Sage, best friend and fellow cohort.

"This better be good," I answered. "I'm wet and naked and with a man."

A brief pause stretched before he answered. "Oh really? Who's the lucky guy?"

"Mr. Bubbles."

He chuckled after another pause. "Had me going for a minute, Des."

"Good. Did you get my message about Thomas Whitcomb?"

"Yeah. Good work. His brother, Charles, never left his house the entire day."

"Damn, Nick, you should've called me. I'd've relieved you at some point."

"Cussing bowl, one buck."

"Shit!"

"Make that two." Over a smile he couldn't see, I growled into the receiver.

He laughed and we discussed the Whitcomb brothers, ventured to the Reynolds's case and how it progressed nowhere fast. As Nick mentioned rechecking bus and train ticket purchases for the day of Sarah's disappearance, the bathroom door—the very locked bathroom door—opened and in strode Armand. He looked as if he possessed not one tiny qualm over invading my privacy.

"Get out!" I barked. (Why did I even bother? I knew he wouldn't leave.)

"What?" Nick asked.

"Not you," I said. Armand perched on the tub's edge. My lip curled and I gave him a vicious look through mean, narrowed eyes that said retribution was soon forthcoming. Did the man not know I owned guns? I covered the phone and hissed, "Leave!"

I heard Nick's, "Who's there?" a second before Armand's, "Hang up."

With a glare at Armand, I sank farther under the bubbles and told Nick, "I have to go and teach someone some manners. Sorry."

"If you need any help disposing of the body, just yell." I heard the smirk in his voice loud and clear.

"When I'm done with him, what's left will most likely resemble Kibbles 'n Bits so I'll just use the garbage disposal, but thanks for the offer."

"Seriously, you okay?"

"Hunky-dory."

"Yell if you need me."

"Roger Wilco."

I tossed the phone on my pile of clothes and opened my mouth but Armand held up his hand to waylay my snarl. He sighed. "I don't know how best to say this."

I didn't like his tone of voice; it hinted of bad things ahead. "What?"

He raked a careless hand through his hair. "It's Penelope."

My heart rate tripled before he managed to finish her name's fourth syllable. I choked, "What's wrong? Where is she?"

His hand swam in the water and grasped mine tight. "She's fine," he assured. His eyes, though, said differently.

"Where is she?" I repeated. Pictures of emergency rooms flashed through my mind—operating tables, spurting blood, code reds. My nails dug into his hand. "Tell me."

"Damian has her."

At his name, my mind emptied and turned vacant, like a playground at night. Wrinkling in my bath water under a thick blanket of Mr. Bubbles, I stared blankly at Armand.

"Did you hear me?" he asked, concerned. "Damian Bochere has taken your aunt."

My picnic dinner of chicken, corn bread and baked beans rose in my throat and tried to crawl out. I attempted to swallow and my eyes burned, my head swam round in fast, dizzy laps.

"*Non!*" he commanded, grabbing my shoulders. He spoke with his nose close to mine. "Is this how you'll help her?" He tightened his grasp: "You lay here feeling sorry for yourself while your aunt needs you?"

Anger pushed aside the other dozen or so emotions writhing within me and wrath tightened in my chest like a titanium fist. I asked a question I already knew the answer to. "What does he want?"

Armand's lips curved in a humorless smile, his eyes seared into mine. "You, *mon chou*, and me."

"I'm going to kill the bastard."

His lips twisted. "You'll have to dry off first."

* * * * *

I helped pull the bed about a foot from the wall and spread our combined rocks and crystals around the room's perimeter. "I still say this is wasting time! We should just go!" I sounded disgruntled and slightly insane, which was exactly how I felt.

Armand looked at me from where he kneeled with his candle. "I have explained this to you. If we arrive unprepared, we'd be no more able to save your aunt or ourselves than helpless children would. This is necessary. We have until midnight." He poured his hocus-pocus blue liquid into the candle's well.

Damian had abducted Aunt P; I accepted it as truth, a horrifying fact. As a stoic Armand watched I'd checked the entire house, room by room, and stood in her empty bedroom, accepted he was right. She was gone.

He'd returned from the restaurant's men's room to find a note sitting at their table in place of Aunt P. The words he read so stirred his anger that before he left, he ripped up the note, tossed the torn bits on the table.

Damian assured the safety of my aunt if we met him at midnight under the full moon. Supposedly. The note instructed us how to find him; Armand would take me there. We'd battle, two against one, and save the day. That was the plan.

"How can we trust him? Who's to say he'll keep her safe till midnight?" I paced and ranted. My gaze kept swinging to my clock's fluorescent hands, inching toward ten o'clock.

Armand stood. "We can't trust him, but there's no benefit in harming Penelope."

"Since when do psychopaths need benefits?"

An enveloping hug stopped my pacing and he spoke soft reassuring words near my ear. "She'll be fine, hold yourself together. You're not alone; I'm with you now. We'll save her." His lips brushed my temple once, then again, lingering there in a soliciting nuzzle. "Are you ready?"

He'd explained earlier about our preparation while I half-listened to phrases like 'poles of power' and 'forming a gestalt' and 'primary merging ritual'. Bottom line? It didn't matter what was to come. I'd do anything to save Aunt P. Anything. Whether that be wrestling alligators, leaping tall buildings, or even mumbling magical incantations with a French witch.

"Yeah, I'm ready." I looked up at him. "This is the only way?"

He cupped my cheek. "*Non*, this is just the best way." He led me to the pentagram he'd made by pouring sand on my carpet (I hadn't even winced at the sight) and the waiting candle placed in its center.

Chapter 24

It was a nasty case of déjà vu. We sat on the floor holding hands over an unlit candle. I frowned. Racing winds screaming in my ears and pictures flying off my walls did not a happy memory make, nor was the feeling of my magic itself what I'd term as pleasant. No, because truthfully, it didn't feel like it belonged to me. Aggressive and dominant was my mojo, pushy, almost like a separate entity encased within my skin...and perhaps unhappy there. Did it obey me or I it? Control was just one of a multitude of concerns that tied my stomach in a hard knot.

"Light the candle, *mon chou*."

I looked at the white molded wax, its dark wick, the small pool of blue liquid sitting calm within its well, and gnawed the inside of my mouth. The sharp sting felt reassuring and staved hyperventilation.

Like flinging wide a hidden door or flipping an unseen switch, I focused my energy and opened myself to magic. Power tingled along my spine and something slithered inside me, waking strong and eager. I thought the word 'Light' and the candle flamed. Hair still damp from bath water lifted and danced on the sudden swell of a warm breeze as the crystals surrounding us blazed to life.

"*Bon*, good," Armand said. "We'll begin. Repeat my words: *We are one mind and spirit, me and thee, together when apart, near when far, will joined to will, thoughts within thoughts, bound as one, as we will, so mote it be.*"

All the while I spoke his words, power roiled within me, climbing higher and higher, like advancing rungs on a ladder, pulsing and pressing inexorably. Shuddering, I moaned with its force.

Armand counseled, "Don't fight it, be as one."

If I could have managed a snort, it would have been a long sarcastic one because he asked of me the impossible—to surrender what was me, my essence, and willingly become something else. Something unknown.

My magic called for Armand, for his long hair moving in the breeze, his eyes, unnaturally black, shadowed with sensuality and heat while boring into mine, his nose, the nostrils flaring, his firm lips, parting. Hunger flared, stinging sharp, submerging me in need.

I swam in magic and arousal. Again I moaned.

"*Oui, suivez-moi*," he crooned, running his thumbs over my knuckles.

My eyes closed at the hypnotic sound of his voice, his touch, and my lessening resistance to the surging, brilliant thrill of flooding energy. My eyes opened and I ordered, "Speak English."

His mouth curved in a sensual smile and he spoke three simple words. "Come to me."

Want swamped me, every cell, every pore, every microscopic atom; I breathed it in and out like a fine heady mist, and with a thought, extinguished the candle between us, sent it flying across the room to thud against a wall.

I found myself in his arms without knowing how I got there, my lips rubbing his, tongue slicking tongue, hands caressing each other's hair. Our powers flared, soared, and tamping a scream, I released a heavy groan as his power, a decidedly masculine energy, swirled inside me. My magic welcomed it eagerly.

Mouths still locked, he drew me up, backed me toward the bed. Everything felt heightened, my wants, my needs, desires, even anger, and it didn't all originate from me. *It* wanted him, that thing writhing inside me.

One clear thought emerged, an instant of sanity where my legs locked and I pushed in denial against his shoulders.

He broke the kiss to murmur, "It has to be. The spell demands it."

Well, he'd neglected to mention that fine little tidbit. I managed a glare before he swooped and redoubled his quest of kissing me senseless. He needn't have bothered; I was already there.

We grappled with each other's clothes. Buttons popped. Material ripped. Armand flicked an impatient finger and my lingerie disappeared. Instantly. Never to be found again. It was my favorite set, too.

His gaze burned along my nude form and settled on the full swell of my breasts. He groaned, "*Mon Dieu.*" I couldn't linger under his stare; magic beat at me in angered impatience, compelling action that very second.

Dropping to my knees, I trailed my nails down his stomach, and watched ten faint lines darken red upon his flesh while hard muscles bunched and clenched on my way to lower things. My fingers wound around the perfection of him, his cock's hard length springing tall and thick from its curly nest. My tongue tunneled in his wet slit. Warm and exciting was his flavor, rich and tangy and full. My eyelids fluttered closed and within me from head to toe, dizzy tingles pricked.

Armand gave a deep-throated moan, then another, the second somewhat broken, before cradling my head. At his cock's thick base, my right hand slicked up and down while my left massaged his tight balls. I licked his sensitive ridge, swirling my tongue around its rim, teasing with small nibbles, then filled my mouth with cock.

His husky cry roughened near its endnote into a deep growl and he drew me to my feet, murmured something foreign, something wicked I'm sure, before pressing his body flush in a sizzling burn.

Armand's mouth crushed to mine. He tangled his hands in my hair, gathering curls within his palms, and plunged his tongue between my parted lips. I stood on tiptoes and smoothed my leg up his, curling it around his hip, lifting my pelvis high in a circling grind against his hard length. His cock felt like an iron rod trapped between our bodies and the balls in his sac were hard, hot, and drawn taut. Our pubic curls brushed together.

The power inside me spiked, rejoiced.

Armand broke the kiss and stared at me with eyes gone wild. His hands grazed the curves of my breasts before cupping their weight in a soft squeeze, plucking my nipples, sending roiling heat to my belly. I shivered, gasped. Around to my back his hands slid, caressing hot down my spine to cup and squeeze my ass before grasping the backs of my thighs. He lifted.

My hands latched onto his shoulders, my legs—his waist, and I wrapped my body around him like a warm supple vest. Encircling us, the wind whispered and pulsed.

With rhythmic squeezes he kneaded my thighs, circled his rocking hips, and pushed his cock between my legs where it poked, prodded, and slid against saturated hairs. The tease was too much.

"Now!" I panted.

"*Oui*, now."

I reached between us and caught it, long hot steel, sizzling within my palm, and he drove his hips upward. Spearing pressure filled me, stiff and full, as I shuddered, biting deep into his shoulder. A satisfied grunt sounded near my ear, sending goosebumps in a rampant, tingling flight down my arms, and he began to thrust with a searing, brisk pace. Solid lunges, long wet glides, raw and powerful, his chest hair tickling my breasts, the very smell of him, drew from me rhythmic cries. Energy surged as our powers electrified.

I found myself kissing his neck, laving there, biting, and pumping wild and wanton on his cock. He toppled us to the bed with me trapped beneath.

His body rocked on mine, in mine, flesh sliding along flesh, slapping and grinding, cock plowing between my thighs. Words were spoken. Requests made. All fell on deaf ears; I was lost. Armand's hips stilled and his teeth grasped my bottom lip and bit down. My eyes widened and focused.

"Repeat it," he demanded.

"Fine!" How he expected me to concentrate at a time like that I didn't know. And certainly, had I known then what I know now, this is the very part I should have skipped. It finished the ritual, sealed it up nice and tight with a shiny bow on top, and caused nothing but trouble. Damn him. *"We are one body,"* I said, *"me and thee, together when apart, touching when separated, flesh of the same flesh, as we will, so mote it be."*

The room's breeze gusted once, then calmed. The words set my insides on fire, a flash of burning liquid like spilled hot wax, and before a pained gasp bounded loose, the heat banked to a slow pulsing warmth, a mere whisper of power and shared knowing.

We joined not only our bodies. Sex I know (okay, admittedly I'm no Cosmo girl, but I do all right), and although it can certainly be wonderful, this was just so far beyond plain wonderful. This was...extraordinary. All that we were, powers and needs and wants, our very essences, swirled and settled into an all-encompassing union, a unique merging. I *knew* him, recognized him as part of myself. Together, one entity. Warm, salty tears leaked down my temples as I quivered.

Armand licked my stinging lip. "You're beautiful, inside and out. You're part of me now. Do you feel it?"

"Yes."

He kissed me, sweet and intense, took my hands, linked our fingers, and moved in me with long, sensuous thrusts. My legs wrapped around him, shaky against his firm flesh, as I felt each glide of his cock, hypnotic and vigorous, molten, plunging back and forth in slippery friction. I dug my heels into his flesh, raised my pelvis at each stroke's end to feel his every thick centimeter while tension twisted and pulled; pressure built high, made all the more intense with the bold stare of his jet eyes. The moments held meaning, power, union...and magic.

Armand groaned, surged his cock from long slow thrusts to brisk urgent plunges, and coaxed, "*Jouir*, come *mon* Desy, *jouir*." His voice rolled through me in smooth velvet waves, beguiling, overflowing my very pores with lust and pleasure.

I drew a catchy breath of surprise, clenched my legs around him, and held his gaze as I rocketed over the edge, the ensuing pleasure forcing a sob from my throat while my hips twisted and bucked. I burst in hard rippling swells that deepened and multiplied, washing over me in pulsating, fevered spasms. Inside me magic whirled.

With eyes closed Armand threw back his head, shouting a hoarse cry, and with hips jerking, cock jumping, he poured into me, thick and scalding, before collapsing with a sharp gasp of my name. He felt heavy and good...and right.

On my exhale I breathed, "Vive la France."

Chapter 25

Except for being very, very aware of him, even more so than previously (which I would have thought impossible), with my magic quiet I felt no different after the spell than before it. Supposedly it combined our powers, essentially doubling them, making us stronger and better prepared for what was to come with Damian. I had my doubts.

I turned to Armand in my Jeep. "Shouldn't I feel different…uh, after the spell, I mean?…because I don't, and it has me worried."

At his insistence, he drove us over wet roads to where Damian held Aunt P as the rain slowed to a fine spraying mist. I sat on the passenger side of the Jeep, a first for me, and looked at his strong profile, asking question after question that night's drive, at least twenty minutes' worth.

"I've never performed it before, I don't know how you're supposed to feel. I only know it succeeded. Trust in me." He took his eyes off the road for a second and looked at me. "*Mon chou*, don't worry so." (Easy for him to say, it wasn't his aunt who'd been abducted.)

Sighing, I shifted to a more comfortable position and rifled through my glove box, finding nothing but an excess of fast food napkins and maps. Sighing again, I pushed the compartment's door shut and resumed tap, tap, tapping my foot on the floor mat.

Doom hung around my shoulders in a heavy fatalistic cape. Even though I was armed to the teeth that night, even though I'd participated in some kind of hocus-pocus strength booster, like some type of giant magical pill, even though I could bench press nearly my own weight and execute a quite impressive high kick,

I still felt a sense of murky futility. And I didn't like it. Not one bit. So I set my shoulders and mentally sneered at it. Scoff! Scoff! Scoff! Everything was fine.

Peppering Armand with endless questions and battling my internal dialogue proved a nice distraction. I glanced at my watch, a Rolex knockoff with faux diamonds (cheesy, but I like it), and read 11:35 as Armand pulled into a driveway.

Unfortunately, it was an all too familiar one.

"You've got to be kidding!" I yelled, twisting in my seat to watch as he maneuvered into a parking spot. "Tell me you're kidding. You're just lost, right?" I slapped my leg. "I told you I should drive!"

He turned off the ignition, unhooked his seatbelt and observed what I can only assume were my eyes bugging from their sockets like a cartoon character's. "This is where the note said to find Penelope. Is there a problem?" Unconcerned, nonchalant even.

I sucked in a calming breath that didn't quite do the job. I felt anything but calm. Dismayed maybe, incredulous, horrified certainly, but not calm. "You're sure?"

"*Oui.*" He opened his door and slid out. When I didn't follow suit, he peered inside at me. "Coming?"

We were in the parking lot of Club Wicked. And as if that wasn't enough (and it was, believe me), my mind already jumped ahead and made the astonishing discovery (better late than never) that in all likelihood, my Grand High Poobah was one Damian Bochere—parental murderer and bug lover extraordinare.

Lucky, lucky me.

And it's funny how your mind works, too. Something about his voice bothered me no end the previous night but I couldn't quite put my finger on it. Well, when it was too late, my brain served up the answer on a silver platter festooned with self-mockery. He spoke with an accent. A French one.

I focused on Aunt P, threw open my door, flung it shut with a vicious, satisfying slam, and stalked toward the entrance. "C'mon," I called over my shoulder. "You coming?"

* * * * *

Armand didn't have to pay at the door. The bouncers took one look at him and let us both cut in line to enter free-of-charge. I doubted it was his outrageous good looks or charming personality (although he has an excess of both). No, Nick would've been let in for free the previous night if that was the criterion. It was as if they recognized him, and that sizzling speculation dropped an uneasy seed to rest heavy in my gut.

I set my shoulders and scoffed. Everything was fine.

When he grasped my hand and led me without hesitation through the dancing mass of sweaty teens, strobe lights, and excessive perfume directly toward the hallway I raced down the night before, that uneasy seed sprouted and grew. Dug in roots.

I set my shoulders and scoffed. Everything was fine.

Sure-footed and silent, Armand turned left in the hall and headed straight to the VIP room. No stopping for directions. No pausing. That seed shot up tall, spread shoots, doubled in size. My belly writhed with it.

I set my shoulders and scoffed. Everything was fine.

When we stood outside the VIP door and he calmly placed his thumb on the print reader, and it flashed a mocking green before he led me inside, what started as a small seed bloomed ponderous in my stomach, thick and weighty, and tried its best to crawl up my throat. I swallowed it down, twice.

Inside, right after I heard the soft click of the door behind me, my shoulders drooped and I scoffed at all my scoffing. Everything was so very much not fine. Not fine at all. Nope.

We stood together in the semi-darkness and my mind jumped from conclusion to conclusion, all dirty, wet and slippery, as if leaping on slimy lily pads atop an endless black lagoon, and I found myself at a place completely unexpected: betrayed and alone.

I asked my questions in a small voice devoid of life. "There never was any restaurant, was there? Or a note, right?" I aged years before his pause mere seconds in length. "*Non*," he whispered. That one word, innocuous in and of itself, sliced me open. The pain stung sharp, palpable.

He led me to the railing, the one I remembered gripping so hard my handprints must surely have imprinted on the steel. "You're part of his coven?" He squeezed my hand and the gesture made me realize he still held it. I yanked it loose and he sighed. "Not *exactement*."

Not exactly!? Not exactly!? As in, 'Gee Desy, your still-beating heart wasn't *exactly* ripped from your chest and thrown on the ground—it just sort of slipped and fell.' That type of not exactly? I wondered.

He pointed downwards. "Damian is below, there, in the black robe."

I looked down and saw my Grand High Poobah, directing his coven in the lighting of candles, a Wiccan micro-manager. I didn't see Aunt P and sent up a quick prayer that she was all right, although if quick prayers actually worked, Armand would have already been struck dead by lightning.

"It's not what you think," he said.

Right. A little puff of air escaped my lips, a mixture of anger and shock and frustration topped off with a high rounded scoop of just plain ol' hurt.

In my little part of the world, truth is not elastic, and anyone trying to stretch it, like my fine Frenchman that night, is nothing more than a liar and not worth my time (except of course if your job requires you to tell lies occasionally, just little white ones mind you, like mine does, then it's acceptable). What you don't do is lie to or betray your friends…or people you just rolled around nude with on 320 count, floral cotton sheets.

I sighed. My intuition screamed when I first met Armand and again that night while riding with him in my Jeep. I'd disregarded both instances. Next time I do that, ignore my intuition, I wish someone would just knock me upside my head, a real good one, too, and smack some sense into me. But on Saturday night it was just too late. I didn't have to be a sanitation engineer to smell all the French garbage floating my way.

"Don't be fooled by his appearance," Armand noted. "Those angelic looks are just trickery." He should talk. Since he seemed a leading expert on the subject, I peered down at Damian again and saw the same normal Joe from the previous night—a big honker of a nose, receding hairline—there was nothing angelic about him.

Perplexed, I ordered, "Define angelic."

Armand touched my arm, I jerked away, and following a slight hesitation, he answered, "The long blond hair, his youth, the shining white aura surrounding him—"

"What are you talking about?" I gave him a glance that asked if he'd lost his mind. Unfortunately, it went to waste; the balcony was just too dark to see more than shadows. "Did you lose your sight along with your conscience? He's got a nose that's been busted more than once, he's 50 if he's a day, and good ol' Damian there will soon have more hair sprouting on his back and ears than on his head."

I scanned below for Aunt P.

"He's under a glamour spell. How can you see him true?"

"Maybe because I'm keenly perceptive and you're dense as a brick?" (Although that wasn't entirely true or I would have dropkicked his handsome ass days ago).

"We should go down. Remember, trust in me, things are not all what they appear."

You're goddamned right they're not, I thought. "You know, you must have missed a spot—it stings less than you'd think."

"Stings?"

Heading for the stairs, I walked around him and hissed, "Yeah, this knife in my back!"

Chapter 26

We stood on one side of the pentagram, Armand and I, while on the other stood Damian and his followers. The hazy eyes of each coven member were unfocused; the effect of his binding spell I supposed. Were they even aware of what transpired around them? I wondered.

"Ah good, Armand, you brought her to me."

Just before crossing to Damian's side, Armand spoke to me in a whisper. "Forgive me."

When hell freezes over. When pigs fly. When...well, you get the idea.

My head swam in fuzzy tingles and my gut felt worse than road kill. Nevertheless, I crossed my arms in front of me in a loose hold, a nonchalant stance, as if to say I could handle whatever came my way—easier than swatting flies or spittin' tobacco. Did I have anyone fooled?

"Where's my aunt?" I asked of Damian, and prayed my voice sounded brave and strong rather than the quivering pathetic snivel I actually heard echo in my own ears. I resisted the urge to gnaw the inside of my mouth bloody.

"Introductions first, although you'll forgive me for not realizing it was you last night. Your appearance has since greatly improved," he said with a smile. "Do you know who I am?"

Was his disparaging reference to last night's hair gel and nose ring? And did I care? I made a little sound of annoyance. "I'll take Who Is Damian Bochere? for 50 please." My lips curved as his straightened to a fine line. Armand winced.

"You're impudent, Desdemona. I believe it must be an inherited trait." He smiled again. "From your parents...both deceased, yes?"

Bulls-eye. 100 points. Ding! Ding! Ding! My heart twisted and before I could stop it, my gaze slid to Armand. He looked stoic, unemotional. Bully for him.

Damian glowered at my lack of response before smoothing his expression. "Bring her aunt. She should watch the show." Two of his coven left the room and two others moved from the group's rear to take their place behind him. One was a girl and the light of three dozen or more candles flickered on her face — Sarah Reynolds, unmistakably.

The rapid beat of my heart kicked up another notch at the confirmation, although the knowledge stung bittersweet. I'd found the teen and solved the case but it was unlikely I'd live to tell about it. How was I to explain it to Sarah's parents anyway? "Uh, Mr. and Mrs. Reynolds, your daughter has been held magically enslaved these past two weeks under a binding spell by a High Wiccan Priest from Paris, France." Snort. That would go over real well.

Regardless, my burden just grew heavier — not only did I have to rescue my aunt, but in addition one, perhaps more, wayward teenaged witches as well. The odds weren't all that great, in fact, pretty dismal.

I succumbed and chewed on the inside of my mouth, tissue there raw and bunched. Pain sliced sharp, and conversely, helped calm me. Somewhat.

To my right, two witches escorted Aunt P into the room. She stared straight ahead; Damian's binding spell shone in her hazed blank expression. A small cry broke from my lips seeing her like that. Where was her happy expression? The twinkle in her eyes? I took a step toward her, then another.

Damian raised his arm. I plowed into a solid barrier, an invisible brick wall, and stumbled backwards, rubbing my nose. My fingers met something wet. Blood. Damn.

I swiped at it and concentrated on my aunt, who still wore her fluorescent housedress; the orange material wrinkled and creased. Dressed for a nice dinner out with our trustworthy houseguest? Obviously not. That meant Armand took her to the club soon after I left on my date. Had everything been a lie with him? Every word? Every action? Every emotion I read on his face and in his eyes? All just pretense and manipulation?

Anger speared within and I turned with fisted hands to the two masculine, French thorns in my side. I expected this of Damian—he was a murderer, a power-hungry demented psychopath. Loony. Armand was a different story. We'd welcomed him into our home, Aunt P and I. I'd welcomed him into my bed.

My back arched with tingling power. I hadn't called or reached for it and its surprise arrival stunned me, making my breath hitch. Anger fed it, my sorrow and betrayal strengthened it, until I felt magic running free in heady exultation throughout every fiber of my being. My flesh trembled.

Unconcerned, Damian chuckled. "Armand, *mon ami*, I do believe we have angered the little priestess, have we not?"

Armand replied, "*Mon ami*? *Non*. I am no friend of yours." He spoke to Damian while watching me.

A grin lit Damian's face as he glanced at Armand. "No," he agreed, "but you will obey me. Shall I tell your friend why?" Sly, that's how he sounded. Conniving. Full of himself and overflowing.

"Do as you will."

Damian tsked and turned to me. "I have played you both," he boasted, "and frankly, found it not much of a challenge." His expression said he pitied us being so far beneath him both in power and intellect. "Armand was the only one who knew of your location. In order to find you, I had to control him; it was simply done." He shrugged his shoulders. "Not only am I the stronger witch, I'm also in possession of someone he loves."

Damian snapped his fingers and from the room's darkened edge a young girl emerged. "Desdemona, I'd like to present Giselle Bellamy, Armand's sister."

I recognized that wholesome face, knew that glossy black hair shining nearly blue in the candlelight. She was Damian's intended virginal sacrifice of Friday night, the girl I'd tried to save before he sicced on me the equivalent of an entomologist's wet dream.

Dressed in jeans and a pink blouse, she stared with glazed eyes at Damian and stalwart, eyes intense, Armand stared only at her.

Guess that explained his cryptic comment of, "Things are not what they seem." He'd done what he'd done to protect his sister. I understood better. Still, a line had been drawn in the pentagram, so to speak, and he wasn't standing on my side of it.

I tucked my hands beneath my arms to hide their constant shaking. "If you're holding her to coerce Armand, why were you going to skewer her last night?"

Damian's expression glared calculating and unpleasant. "Armand had a simple job—get you here under the full moon any way he could. He informed me last night he'd failed. I felt his sister's death a proper punishment."

Near the end of Damian's words, Armand's gaze caught mine and his eyes held magic in their black depths. He spoke to me then, simple words really, but they shocked me more than anything he'd done yet that night.

Why, you ask? Good question.

His lips didn't move. He spoke to me using his mind.

Mon chou, are you listening? He will strike soon. I'll handle him, but you must get Penelope and Giselle to safety.

I froze. Ventriloquism? Not hardly. Whatever he'd done to me in my bedroom, that spell, repeating all those damn words, somehow granted him free access to my mind. I wanted to scoff at the thought—after all, it seemed so ludicrous—but I'd done plenty of scoffing that night and all it did was land me in a shitload of trouble.

Desy?

I stared at him through narrowed eyes. *Yeah, yeah, I hear you, and if I live through this, I'm going to make your life a living hell.* I knew he heard me loud and clear when he had the audacity to wear a slight smile.

I look forward to it.

Damian finished crowing and I tried to reason with him, figuring it couldn't hurt. "I don't want any part of your council, I'll never challenge your leadership, you have my word. Doesn't that make any difference?"

"No, you're of the line. And now it's time to say our good-byes."

With that closing statement, his eyes turned deep black, like a shade pulled, and over me rushed a wave of his power, reminiscent of the previous night's, wicked and just plain wrong, but on a much stronger level because it had a target. Me.

I felt another power — Armand's. His magic rose within me and joined with my own. The forces rejoiced, melded, and inside me the energies swelled.

Damian chanted foreign gibberish in a melodious voice, saying what I was sure were perfectly horrible things. Feet lifting off the ground, he levitated, floating in midair. It was an astonishing, frightening sight and had I been alone with him, I'd have darted for the nearest exit. But Aunt P kept me there, and Sarah Reynolds, and Giselle, and all right, even Armand, although he hardly deserved it.

Candlelight flickered off Damian's black robe, danced in his raven eyes, and a dozen monotone voices echoed his words. A cold breeze swept the room, arched up my spine, sending goosebumps scampering, and like my flesh, the cement floor trembled. The cloying scent of poppies filled my nostrils, curling through the air thick enough to make my head spin. Eerie didn't begin to describe his magic.

Damian pointed at me. A blue streak of light flashed lightning quick and just as dangerous.

Armand roared, "No!" He dived forward...and took the hit for me.

Chapter 27

A screamer I'm not. Usually the most you'll get from me at say a scary movie is a wince or slight cringe, but that night fear grabbed me by the throat in a throbbing bruise and the air shook with my screams. I managed to belt out two as Armand thudded to the floor, rolled to his side and moaned beneath Damian's sick laughter.

Damian pointed at the new target, his downed adversary, and I started toward Armand with no idea how to help; I just knew he was in pain. He lay curled slightly in on himself, face pulled in a clammy grimace. I took a couple steps, then heard his strident voice.

Non! Run! Run!

The men began to battle like a mystical shootout, targeting power down their arms and releasing it. Between them fierce blue lightning arced. Armand held his own against Damian but it was obvious who was the more powerful. The knowledge shone on Damian's face in maddened glee. Only a matter of time before Armand tired…and failed. I stood frozen with the sick insight.

Run!

I did, pivoted away from escalating chants, candles' flames dancing in the room's cold breeze; I turned from violent blue beams, their energy silent but deadly, and ran from a levitating madman as Armand lay hurt on the ground fighting for his life.

I rushed to my aunt and Giselle and led them from the room. They walked in a trance's pace, slow but willing, and I prayed I'd get them out before Damian noticed.

The stairs leading to the club's main floor were too visible. A short hall led to what I hoped was a back exit and I yanked open the door, sobbed with relief. Concrete steps gave way to a small rear parking lot. Empty. The rain had stopped and the night snapped crisp, the sky twinkled with a shining blanket of stars, and sitting high in its midst blazed a full yellow moon.

Outside, the coven's chanting voices fought against the club's blaring music, the cicadas and tree frogs sang their free nightly concert, and cars zoomed by on Rochester Road. A sharp cry, pained and masculine, pierced the cacophony. Armand.

At the sound, my magic slithered like an impatient snake, and my heart stopped, then pounded. I led Aunt P and Giselle to the wet stairs and eased them down. They stared forward, sitting dutifully in the dampness.

"Stay here," I ordered. "Stay!" Yeah, like that would help.

I raced back inside.

* * * * *

What I know about magic could fill half a Post-it note. Maybe. Shooting beams from my fingers? No idea how. Not a clue. Floating in midair? Binding spells? No and no, haven't the foggiest.

Still, I know something about honor (Aunt P raised me after all) and protecting friends, and although still unsure Armand fell under either category, honorability or friendship, I had to help him.

I skidded back into madness and mayhem to find a levitating Damian with arms outstretched, pelting Armand relentlessly with his power. Armand lay unmoving on the ground, his face pinched and white. His defense, one shaky arm, began to droop under the weight of the attack.

I struggled to call my power through a sheer wall of terror and it surged, writhed. It was ready—I think—the problem was me. I didn't know what to do with it...and the timing couldn't be worse for guessing or practice or bumbling errors. I had to save Armand.

A distraction, that's what was needed, a stalling tactic. "Damian!" I screamed. He focused so strongly to his left where Armand lay, he was unaware of me; I hoped he would pause in his assault and give Armand a chance to breathe...or escape.

Neither happened.

Damian continued his attack on Armand and laughing, pointed one arm at me. I caught a glimpse of his eyes, black and shining with malice, before a blaze of blue shot from his fingertips. I dived, rolled and popped up holding my Springfield .45. Hadn't remembered I'd packed it that night, didn't remember pulling it from its harness. It was just there, in my hand, ready.

I don't know how to shoot magical blue beams, that's true...but I do know how to shoot lead. I aimed at Damian's black heart and pulled the trigger. The sharp retort of the gun reverberated so loud my ears rang. It was a good sound.

Damian jerked and dropped his arms, looked at his chest before slowly raising his head. "What have you done?" he asked, astonished. "Witches don't carry guns."

I smiled. "This one does."

A patch of crimson spread on his chest, barely discernable against his black robe. His shocked gaze met mine and he gasped once before falling to the ground. The sound of his body slapping the cement floor, of his skull as it smacked there, echoed as loud as the gunshot, if not more so. He lay still for no more than a second before disappearing. Yep, that's right. Poof. Gone. No blood. No gore. No Damian.

The chanting ceased, the breeze as well, and the lit candles settled into a soft warm glow.

The gun dropped from my hand to clatter unnoticed on the floor and I hurried to Armand. "Are you okay?" He didn't look it. His eyes were closed, his skin ashen. My heart wrenched and kneeling beside him, I smoothed his hair from his face. "Armand?"

His eyes opened. They were glazed with pain. "You did it."

I smiled through burning eyes gone blurry. It was allergies. "*We* did it," I said.

The mournful sound of sobbing brought my head up. Members of the coven milled about, released from Damian's spell, and the girls hugged, crying into each other's shoulders. The entire group looked distressed. Once freed, I hadn't exactly expected them to break out in a rousing chorus of Kumbaya, but their dour reaction was a bit puzzling.

The oldest member, a man sporting glasses and a goatee, around 40 or so, bowed before Armand and I. His voice was soft. "Thank you."

"Sure," I said and nodded toward the teens. "What's with them?"

"We've been trapped inside our own bodies for—" he raked a hand through his hair "—I don't know how long. We had no control over our actions." He glanced at the teens. "I'm sure they're feeling traumatized. I know I am."

I hummed in agreement and asked his name.

"Sam Bearns." He started to bow again but I held up a hand.

"Are you bowing?"

"Well, yes."

I frowned. "Well don't, and why would you want to anyway?"

Armand whispered, "Because you're a High Priestess, a Queen."

I snorted and eyed Mr. Bearns. "You're the owner of this club, right?"

"Yes...how did you know?"

I fluttered my hand in the air. "Long story. I need you to call 911."

"Would you allow me to help your husband?" he asked.

"Husband?" I squawked. Armand tried disguising his weak laugh behind an equally weak cough. It didn't work.

Mr. Bearns rushed to apologize. "I'm sorry, you're a High Priestess and he's a High Priest and I just assumed—" he pointed to my hand " —with you, uh, rubbing him and all..."

I looked down, realized I smoothed my hand over Armand's chest, back and forth, petting him. My hand stilled and I met Armand's eyes. A mix of pain laced with humor shone in their depths and I yanked back my hand. Shit.

"I can help him, Priestess. My talent is in healing."

"Call me Desy and I'm getting a crick. Bend down."

"Oh! Of course. Forgive me." He kneeled beside me. "May I?" Palms down, he held his hands above Armand's chest.

"You can really help him?"

"Yes."

I looked to Armand. "That okay with you?"

"*Oui.*"

I studied him for a moment, noted his pallor, and motioned for Mr. Bearns to proceed. On my way toward Sarah Reynolds, each teen I passed bowed, causing a frown to work at my mouth. When a hard pounding reached my ears, I stilled and cocked my head. Fists against steel. I smiled.

Aunt P wanted back inside.

Chapter 28

Damian Bochere is a madman involved in the occult, who lured unsuspecting teens (and one club owner) to join him, then drugged them. When I happened to track him down during my investigation of Sarah Reynolds's disappearance, he pulled a gun on me and I shot him in self-defense. He ran away to parts unknown, possibly injured, but very much alive.

At least, that's the story conveyed to the police.

The Wiccan bunch is quite a tight little group and with a straight face, each coven member repeated the same fairytale. The police bought it and issued an APB for Mr. Bochere's sorry ass. I wished them luck.

Was he dead? Did I kill him? Don't know, not for sure really. Disappearing bodies can do that to you...cast doubt and open a whole can of 'What in the hell just happened?' All I knew that night with any certainty was everyone was safe, and I had one less case to worry about.

* * * * *

"The police still have more questions for me. Can you take Aunt P with you to your house?" I called Nick from the club before dialing up the good men in blue. He arrived soon after they did and never left my side.

His eyes were an alert lively blue for three a.m. "My house? Why don't I just take her home?"

"Yes, I'd like to hear the answer to that question myself," Aunt P said from my left. Beside her stood Armand and his sister, holding hands. My glance took them all in and I frowned.

"Desy doesn't trust me around you now, Penelope," Armand commented. "Isn't that right, *mon chou*?" Sam Bearns had performed his healing mumbo-jumbo and Armand stood hale and hearty watching me. After a moment, he sighed. "Giselle and I will stay in a hotel. I'll send someone over for my things."

I said, "That would be best," as Aunt P stated a firm, "Absolutely not," and over our clashing voices Nick asked, "What's going on?"

Nick's presence hampered truth. I stood in a dull rainbow, stuck in murky grays between the more straightforward blacks and whites, unable to say what really happened and how I'd arrived at my decision to disallow anything of French origin near my aunt again. Ever.

"Nick," Aunt P said. "Could you please get me a glass of water?"

Nick's sharp gaze traveled over our small group. "Sure. About ten minutes' worth?"

Aunt P smiled. "Yes, dear." When he was out of earshot, she turned to me. "Armand is welcome in our home. Giselle will stay in the bedroom across from mine." Her voice rapped matter-of-fact and the tone told me distinctly not to argue. Distinctly. Fat chance.

"Do you not understand what happened tonight? That man—" I jabbed a finger toward Armand "—abducted you. You could have been hurt! We all could have—"

"He didn't abduct me."

My outrage sagged a bit. "What do you mean he didn't abduct you? Of course he did." I looked at Armand and couldn't read his expression. Giselle watched us quietly, her beautiful face solemn.

"I came willingly. Insisted on it, actually. He explained everything to me and I felt it was the only way. Damian had to be stopped. Giselle had to be rescued." My aunt looked as calm as if she just commented peaches have fuzz.

"My head hurts…you…he…" I floundered and dragged a hand over my face. My nose throbbed less than my hurt feelings. "You willingly came here in order to…to manipulate me into fighting that madman?"

I cringed when she scolded, "Desdemona Adeline Chantal Phatt!" (She only uses my full name when she's hot under the collar.) Aunt P continued in a chilled tone. "Of course not! You're an adult. You chose not to involve yourself and I respected that." Then more softly, "I came here tonight to try to talk some sense into that Damian person…and well, he just wouldn't listen. It didn't work out as I hoped."

Ah, but it had for Armand. I met his gaze. "Why didn't you just tell me Aunt P came here to stop Damian? Why the lie about the restaurant and note?"

"Do you really want to discuss this now?" he asked.

My hands landed on my hips. "Yeah, I really want to discuss this now."

"Very well. Would you have been…pleased with me had you known I brought Penelope here to confront Damian?"

"Pleased?" I snorted. "Not hardly."

He nodded. "In order to perform the merging spell, both partners must be…amenable. It wouldn't have worked had you entered it in anger or resistance. I had to ensure that your hostile feelings centered not on me, but on Damian."

"By lying."

His lips tightened a fraction. "We saved many lives tonight with that lie."

My shoulders sagged. "Sweetie pie," Aunt P said, "we'll take a cab home." She patted my arm. "Don't stay too long. And drive carefully."

Armand held the Jeep's keys aloft. "Keep them," I said. "Nick will drive me home or I'll hitch a ride in a squad car." I looked at Aunt P. "I don't like this. You're sure?"

She smiled and patted my arm again. They left, but not before Giselle unexpectedly hugged me and whispered, "*Merci beaucoup.*"

✳ ✳ ✳ ✳ ✳

Ecstatic parents picked up Sarah Reynolds after her statement, gushing appreciation to Nick and me, attempting to write out a check right there on the spot. Smiling, I told them we'd soon mail our final bill.

They swept Sarah home. In fact at one point, the entire room buzzed with relieved parents whisking away relieved children...until there was just me, Nick, Sam Bearns, and two officers.

Nick looked at his watch and sighed halfway through the cop's question, which was the same one he'd asked not five minutes past. The patrolman's nametag said Officer A. Barten, but should have said Still-Wet-Behind-The-Ears-Gung-Ho-Rookie. Nick interrupted. "It's going on five a.m. Perhaps Ms. Phatt and I can drop by the station tomorrow and finish this up. She's exhausted."

I eyed Sam. If I looked anything like him, I was a sad sight indeed. He looked dead on his feet.

Officer Remington, a beefy cop with washed-out hardened eyes, spoke. "There's no need." His voice held a touch of twang and drawling lilt, proclaiming a birthplace other than Michigan. "I believe we've got everything." He glanced at his partner's crestfallen face and smirked. "And if it's possible we missed anything, we'll contact you."

"Thanks," Nick said and we watched the officers leave. Tension eased from me and I fought to keep my eyes open. A huge yawn stretched my lips wide and I didn't even bother to cover my mouth. No one should have to practice good manners at five a.m.

Sam asked me, "Is there anything I can do for you, Priestess?"

179

My eyes widened and blazed at him as Nick guffawed. "What did you call her? Priestess?"

Shit.

Sam grasped the situation (a little late) and smacked his forehead with his palm. "Damn. I'm so tired I'm a little loopy. Sorry."

"That's okay," I said in a rush, although it wasn't. "Nick and I are fine. We don't need anything." I looked at Nick hoping to find not speculation on his face, but a nice pleasant blank. Unfortunately, my hope was dashed. He eyed us while his brain whirred. That's all I needed—more questions and more lies. He deserved better. "Can I get a ride home sailor?" I asked him.

"Sure, Des."

We said our good-byes and drove home in silence. I pretended to sleep. He pretended to believe me.

Chapter 29

My hand felt small within his as he led me through the house. French doors were cast open, windows as well, and the night air rushed in warm and fragrant and welcome, fluttering the white silk of my nightgown across my skin with each step. We walked barefoot on wide-planked oak floors skirting lush, elegant furniture. Soft Persian rugs were scattered here and there, soft underfoot, and the glow of faint lighting cast shadows on richly grained woods, soft whites, and Armand's sensual face.

Do you like it, mon chou?

I smiled. *Yes, very much…where are we?*

He gently squeezed my hand. Calluses rested high on his palm, from my garden's shovel, I thought. *My home. I wanted you to see it.*

I sighed, completely relaxed. *It's lovely.*

Double doors opened at his touch to reveal the large master suite. The ceiling curved in a high arch, tall windows flanked a stone fireplace, and in the room's center a massive bed sat dressed in white, topped with several plump pillows.

The breeze brought me jasmine, honeysuckle and evergreen. I inhaled deeply and watched Armand turn down the bed. *Music?* he asked.

Thick carpet sank underfoot as I crossed to a window and looked out into the night. *Sure.* His hand caressed my shoulder, warm and feather-light, before he opened an armoire. Classical music filled the room with soft, dreamy notes. I smiled up at the stars.

You're so very beautiful.

I turned to him. Dressed in a robe of midnight blue, his back to the open armoire, he stood watching me. Chest hair peeked between wide lapels, curling dark on his fair skin, and longer hair, brushing past the robe's collar, framed his sensuous face. The shiny length flowed in a rich temptation; I itched to bury my hands in it. Those classic features, his strong face, drew me and he stared in unguarded fascination as I crossed to him.

You're beautiful too. I said, gaze roaming his face. *I thought so the very first time I saw you.*

Armand smiled down at me. *Did you? And do you know what I thought the first time my eyes met yours?* He brought my hand to his lips, kissed my palm, licked and nibbled at the wet flesh. The look in his eyes sent excited flurries to dance low, swaying in soft, tingling waves within my belly.

No, what did you think?

I thought, my love, that I'd found my destiny, that I must have you. He kissed my palm again, brushed it with a tiny sweep using the wet tip of his tongue. *For life.*

I read the burning intention in his dark eyes and raised up to meet his lips. He moaned at the contact and again when our tongues entwined. It thrilled that I could make this man moan. My fingers threaded through strands of the thick, dark silk on his head and he cupped my butt, pulling me flush, giving a pleased grunt when I rubbed against his erection.

Armand sank deeper into our kiss, sliding his scorching hands along my back and ass, their heat traveling through the silk to burn me. His mouth slid down to lave my jawline and throat while muscles in my belly drew up tight with excitement, and my pulse jolted with a frantic surge of lust.

You're mine. He looked down at me, intense, incredibly so, then his eyes closed with a sweep of jet lashes and he buried his face in my hair, inhaling deep. *Mine. No one else's.*

His words stirred a thought deep inside me that lay buried, disquiet, and my brow furrowed as I reached for it. He leaned back. *Non.* His thumb stroked my forehead, smoothing the crease found there, and he murmured reassurances, soft, soft crooning, until I lost myself in his warmth, his scent, his voice, and the thought simply…faded…away.

Armand eased his fingers under the thin straps of my nightgown and slid them down my arms, holding my gaze as the gown slipped. Silk caressed my breasts and hips as it fell to the floor in a white cloud and with gentle hands, he cupped my face. *You are everything I want, everything I could ever need. Give me a chance. Let me in your life. I can give you so much…magic…my heart…all of me.* His lips brushed my forehead. *And this, mon chou, I can give you this.* He watched me as his lips kissed my nipple, watched me as I puckered there on a shudder and a tingling flush crept along my breasts, coloring the swells pink.

I cradled his head against my breast, tried to breathe as his mouth suckled, firm lips tugging my nipple, wet tongue sliding. When he licked his way across, teased my other nipple into his warm mouth, my legs wobbled, and lifting me effortlessly, he stared into my eyes, carrying me to bed.

The mattress's cushy down cradled with a plush embrace, and he kissed me, stripped off his robe, tossed it on a nearby chair.

He stood nude, gloriously nude and heavily aroused. I held out my arms. *Armand.*

Jesus, you're stunning. Unmatchable. He kneeled above me and rained kisses all over my face.

My hands traced along his broad shoulders and I laughed softly. *What are you doing?*

He breathed his husky answer between kisses pressed along my nose, cheeks and forehead. *Kissing…every…freckle…mon chou…what else?*

My soft laugh bloomed into a chuckle. *That's going to take you a very, very long time.*

His dark eyes met mine. *Exactement.*

Armand's teeth nibbled on my chin before traveling lower, where his mouth and hands moved over me in a mesmerizing path, softly here, pinching there, until I writhed quivering beneath him, needy and throbbing.

He'd teased my nipples into two pulsing points and my breasts throbbed with a pleasurable ache, feeling heavy and full and alive. The recess of my navel tingled from his tongue's wet, thorough exploration, and beneath its veil of brown curls, my mound prickled delightfully from nibbling teeth.

Armand knelt between my spread legs and parted me as gently as the fragile petals of a flower. Two fingers slipped inside. I gasped and he slid them in and out, curling them, scissoring in long sweeps while my heels dug into the mattress with each hips' rotation. He groaned and replaced his fingers with his tongue, plunging it inside me, tunneling deep, burrowing high, and I arched into his mouth; against my drenched lips he hummed rich and low and hungry. My hands grasped the sheet, bunched there in two tight fists, and my eyelids fluttered closed even as my breathing sped to a thick, leaden pant. I shuddered at the delicious feel, the consuming eroticism of his tongue licking inside me.

The room brimmed with soft, lazy tones of piano, the sound of my breathing—heavy and uneven—and wet, juicy moans.

Adept. Skilled. Armand. Within minutes I climbed up, up, up and flew over with a cry. Every nerve and muscle reveled, spiraling in a resonating climax, and before I caught my breath, before my spasms calmed, his cock filled me in one bold thrust. *God!* Armand rasped my name. Hands cupping my sprawled knees, he began pumping inside me, his cock gliding back and forth, driving in thick, fevered suction as pressure built anew.

His hair swung in a dark curtain as he circled his hips, plunging in and out; I grasped two handfuls of it, urging him to lie flat. I wanted his weight, wanted to feel his muscles bunch and work beneath smooth, hot flesh. He murmured his pleasure as he settled on me, skin to skin, and my hands roamed his broad back; my ankles locked there, while Armand laved and sucked my neck.

Every inch of his cock stretched me in searing, bold thrusts and with each plunging upstroke, a ragged mewl leapt from my mouth. I dug my nails into his back; he bit my neck, a welcome pain, as he plowed between my legs. Heat lanced my belly and with a low moan, I stabbed deeper into his flesh, ten half-moons, and the rhythm of our hips sped.

The orgasm broke hard with contractions intense, fierce, so forceful I nearly howled as they spilled in powerful, scalding waves. I couldn't catch my breath enough to moan as Armand's hips pumped a furious set of short strokes. *Christ, Desy!* Inside me thick silk spurt, jetting in warm, abundant streams. With a harsh gasp and shudder, he nuzzled my throat while his hips continued to rock, bobbing his cock in a slow, lazy rhythm. The climax continued, reverberating, rolling me under again in a hard swell, stepping up a notch, and another.

I jerked awake on a scream.

Chapter 30

Dumbfounded, I sat in my bed sweating and panting like a first place thoroughbred at the Kentucky Derby. The sheet clung, twisted tight around me in a choking cocoon. I yanked and spun from it to stand on shaky legs, huffing and slightly dizzy from the effort.

My clock said 2:00 p.m. I crawled into bed that morning around 6:00, feeling half-dead and looking worse. Eight hours of sleep...or sex. I wasn't sure which. My mind whispered I'd just experienced a delicious dream, private, nothing to worry about, but my body screamed that I'd just enjoyed real, mind-blowing, eye-crossing sex. I pondered over which one to listen to.

The dresser mirror revealed huge brown eyes staring back at me, pupils dilated, and hair sticking up on end as if I'd wrestled all night with my pillow and lost.

A white silk nightgown? Don't own one. Men's boxers (my favorite sleepwear) sat twisted on my hips and my stretchy camisole rode bunched and wrinkled at my waist.

Just as I laughed at myself and turned from the mirror, I caught sight of my neck. My mouth fell open at the spectacle. Oh my god. Oh! My! God! That dirty... rotten...son-of-a-bitch! After a shocked pause, I screeched and stalked from my room directly into his without knocking. You don't knock when murder is on your mind.

Armand lay half-propped in bed, weight on one elbow, rumpled, shirtless, and unbelievably appealing. The bastard. A foolish lurch of renewed need, pure lust, bolted through me and I made myself look at him from the neck up only. It was a challenge. His lips twisted at my expression of murderous rage...or perhaps the wild state of my hair; both were quite a sight. "Come in, *mon chou, sil vous plait,* and close the door." He winced at the door's vicious slam. "Before you yip at me," he said, "you must promise you won't rush off in a huff when you hear something you dislike."

Yip? I do *not* yip. "No deal. I can only promise you you'll have one good eye when we're through. Maybe."

He smiled and patted the bed for me to sit. "You're unbelievable!" I ranted, and he looked as disappointed as if he just discovered coal in his Christmas stocking. From the other end of the room I lugged over an overstuffed chair. Aunt P reupholstered it last year in a subdued black and purple stripe with orange fringe. I sat and drummed my fingers on its thick arms, tapped my feet on the carpet, and glared at him through narrowed eyes.

He smiled anew.

"I don't know exactly what you've done with your spell and that...that ritual, but I want you out of my head. Now," I said, stabbing the air with my hand. "No more communicating with just your mind, no more practice sessions in my room, and especially no more hijacking my dreams!"

"Actually," he purred, "that was my dream."

I growled like a maddened, rabid dog. Any moment foam would spill forth from my mouth. Surely that would wipe clean his smile. I snarled, "But it wasn't *just* a dream, now was it, my fine Frenchman?"

"What makes you so sure?" His eyes held a certain spark—a mix of delight, curiosity and humor. If a spark flared in my eyes, it held only mania and homicidal intent.

I whipped my hair up and turned my neck toward him for easy viewing—although the action was hardly necessary—the thing on my neck was the size of a plum and just as colorful. "This, you imbecile!" I jabbed my finger at it. "You gave me a hickey!"

"I prefer to think of it as a love bite." He brazenly smiled again.

I screeched, "I prefer to think of you as dead!" I let my hair fall, leaned back in the chair with a huff.

"*Mon chou*," he admonished with a hand over his heart. "You wound me." I forced myself not to lunge and demonstrate a true wound. Murder One would be an unpleasant conviction. Bunk beds? Orange jumpsuits? Communal showers? Not for me.

"Tell me it won't happen again. Please."

His face turned as serious as my tone. "I'm afraid I can't do that."

I had a feeling he'd say that. Just a hunch. "Explain."

He shifted, sitting up straighter, and the sheet fell lower on his waist. My eyes lingered there before jerking up to meet his warm, intimate gaze. The man should come with a warning sticker, 'View At Your Own Peril'. I clenched my eyes tight and started counting to ten. When I reached seven, he spoke.

"We're joined in a unique way. I'll relate all I know about the spell but the knowledge comes only from what I've read, not true experience. As I've told you, I've never performed it before." He moistened his lips. "We can communicate using mindspeak when we call our power...or when our subconscious takes over during sleep."

"So right now, you can't talk to me with this...this mindspeak?"

"*Non*. Only when both powers are called."

"So we just have to worry about nights for now, right?"

He flashed a wicked smile. "I find nothing worrisome about my nights."

He wouldn't. I frowned. "It doesn't bother you that our dreams are a mix of reality and illusion?"

"What is magic if not the very blend of these two things?"

I squeezed the armrests. "Dream about cars then, or ducks or parades, just leave me out of it! Besides," I reasoned with a shake of my head, "it'll probably all go away when you return to France."

"No one can control their dreams…and I'm not returning to France, at least, not anytime soon."

My heart leapt to my throat. "All right, I'll bite. How long is anytime soon?"

"I've bought a house here…in Pleasant Oaks."

Like a walleye flopping about the shore, my mouth opened and closed, opened and closed. "But that city's only fifteen minutes away!" I sputtered.

"More like ten. You need to be near Penelope—I don't want you traveling far." He smiled. Again.

I ignored his last remark but panic crept into my voice. "You've been here less than a week! When did you buy it?"

His eyes seared into mine with a heady, burning stare, and his voice turned softer than velvet. "The day after I met you."

My heart dropped from my throat to plunge to its rightful spot. "Why? What about Merlin's Attic? What about the covens in Paris—aren't you ruler or High Priest there now?" I speared my hand into my hair and it stuck on a tangled curl. I winced and grabbed onto the armrest again. "And I have a boyfriend. This has all just got to stop!"

Armand bent a leg under the sheet, draped an arm over his knee. "I can run my business from here quite easily; I handpicked my staff and trust them implicitly. Tomorrow Giselle returns to Paris and along with a good friend of mine, she'll oversee the covens there until a better solution arises." He cocked his head. "Forgive me my deception. Please. I tried all other options to rescue my sister before involving you. I saw no other recourse, truly." A smile returned to his face. "And *amoureux*—sweetheart, you don't have a boyfriend. You have a young man with whom you feel…safe. He's not your match. You don't feel challenged or moved. It's—" his smile faded "—disturbing to think of you with him. But soon you'll grow bored; I'll be here when you do."

I opened my mouth but he held up a finger that said Wait, there's more. Oh goody. "You asked why I bought a house here.

The answer is simple—to be near you. I want...I *need* to be at hand when you realize two things."

I could barely breathe and I certainly didn't want to hear about the double something's I'd soon be realizing. I asked anyway. "And what would they be?"

Armand smiled that smile that sets my teeth on edge, the one that seems amused at my expense and slathered with a thick layer of arrogance. "Who but a witch," he said, "can fully accept another witch?"

My lips tightened. "That's only one thing. What's the other?"

His gaze roamed my face, lingered on my mouth before lifting to meet my eyes. Armand's expression burned serious, earnest, and so compelling I forgot to breathe. "Simply this— we're meant for each other, you and I."

With bold intent flashing in his eyes, he flung the sheet aside. Captive air fought its way free from my lungs in a panicked whoosh and I bolted for the door, managing to yank it open a crack before a broad hand appeared above my head and pushed it closed.

Click.

Armand pressed his body flush, curving around me in intoxicating warmth, his cock planted thick and erect in the small of my back. He moved aside my hair, nuzzled the sensitive skin behind my ear. "Always...running...away," he purred in a husky whisper. "Why do you suppose that is? Hmmm?"

A statue, that's what I was, breathless and immobile, without thought, though inside me every cell and nerve quivered.

His hand skimmed along the dark grain of the door to tangle with my fingers on the knob. "It couldn't be from fright." He drew the small lobe of my ear between his lips and released it with a scrape of his teeth. My eyes closed. "*Non*, not my Desy. She's too strong, too confident...fearless." He locked the door.

Click.

Journeying south, Armand's hand left mine to skim under my camisole's hem and dip deep within my shorts. His hand splayed hot and low against my belly. Could he feel the flutters inside? The endless somersaults? The undulating need?

"What would happen do you think," his fingers slipped downward, pressed against my mound, moved soft within its cover of curls, "if you came to me now." He softly plucked at my hairs, root to tip, in an unrelenting mesmerizing tease. "Without cover of night, *mon chou.*" Armand's fingertips ventured between my legs, tugging gently on the wet strands curled around my opening. "With no dreams to hide behind," he whispered. "No magic to push or bolster you."

His cock shifted left to lay thick against my waist and he slid his other hand inside the back of my shorts to fondle the cheeks of my ass. "If you made a conscious decision to be with me." His tongue laved along my throat while skilled fingertips toyed with the drenched hairs between my thighs. One long finger slipped inside the cleft of my ass, smoothing round and round just outside — never quite touching — the puckered rosette hidden there.

I quivered and Armand's lips curved warm against my nape. Chill bumps raced across me, multiplying, and small hairs, almost invisible along my skin, stood. Down my inner thigh, tickling a wet path on my burning flesh, rolled a dewdrop of arousal.

"What would happen if you dropped your guard this once," he breathed in my ear, "and...just...let...go?"

I shuddered with his seductive taunt, the coaxing words, and the knowing tease of his fingers that played near...but never within. I panted. I burned. I wanted. Armand licked the rim of my ear and I jerked my head away.

"That's right — get mad," he whispered. "I'll take you any way I can get you...just as long as you come to me of your own free will."

My eyes opened. "Let me go."

191

He rested his forehead against my temple, kissed my cheek before his hands left me. Against my heated flesh, cool air replaced his body. I turned to find him standing tall a few steps away, cock jutting straight and thick and perfect, black eyes swirling with hunger and cautious hope.

"I'm yours," he said in that sexy, French accent. "Be mine. Come to me."

As fast as it erupted, my anger vanished. His deep voice seduced me with its foreign lilt and persuasive tone; it coaxed, enthralled, lured me. And at his words — "I'm yours" — my heart danced.

I could have unlocked the door and left. I didn't. In that one instance, hindsight was irrelevant; it wouldn't have changed the outcome. Nothing would have.

I pulled my camisole over my head. His eyes flashed, burning brighter. Easing my boxers off, I held his gaze and made my unsteady legs move.

Nude, I walked to him.

Chapter 31

With my name on his lips, Armand enfolded me in a near-crushing embrace. I thrilled to the warmth of his smooth skin, his scent, woodsy and clean, the rapid beat of his heart drumming beneath my ear, and the way his arms wound so tight around me as if he'd never let me go.

I tilted my head, raised on tiptoes to meet his mouth, the kiss fiery and impassioned, yet tender as well. Our tongues rubbed together, tangling in a heated waltz. Eager, his cock bucked against my stomach and I curved my hand around its stiff girth, the thin skin slinking up and down within my moving palm.

Armand pushed a low moan into my mouth. I swallowed it and made it mine, echoing the needy sound as our hips brushed against one another's in a soft grind, a slow erotic dance.

He filled his hands with the cheeks of my ass, kneading, pulling them up and apart with each circling squeeze, curling his fingers in against my anus. Armand backed me toward the bed and, capturing my hands in his, mouth sliding off mine, tongue tracing my jawline, he pressed his lips against my ear. "I love your hands on me. Lie down. I'll return the pleasure."

Our gazes locked tight as he followed me down, and kneeling above me, he drew the tip of my breast deep inside his mouth. My lungs filled fast and sharp. I watched my nipple disappear between his lips, saw his cheeks hollow slightly as he sucked, his teeth flash white as he nibbled, and within me, every nerve sang and danced, bounced and skipped, tugged a fiery path to my clitoris. Armand watched me through hooded eyes.

Between long slow licks, he murmured, "You are…so…damn…beautiful." He shifted up to kiss my lips, his eyes never leaving mine, before moving to my other breast. He suckled. My stomach muscles clenched, and I tangled my hands in his long shiny hair, arched into his mouth. Lust swam thick within me, burning need, while I writhed under him, mindless, rocking against his cock.

Armand nipped at me before rearing up, and as my hands fell empty to the soft mattress, his black eyes flashed. With a growl, in one fluid motion, his hands slid under me, palming my ass, kneading the cheeks, and he buried his face between my spread legs.

I cried out first his name, then several saints' as well.

He nuzzled there, rooting, inhaling deep, and said one word. "Watch."

I eased up on my elbows, my head dizzy with desire, my body throbbing with need, to feel his thumbs slide along my saturated folds, feel myself gently open beneath his soft touch, and witness desire and passion climb higher on Armand's face. Clever hands supporting me, I watched him tip my pelvis up high, as easily as if it were a cup. He drank from me then with greedy swallows, eager gulps, slurping and lapping until a hoarse cry spilled from my mouth, followed by breathy, erratic mewls. I watched him in fascination and widened my spread legs, cupping the backs of my knees over his broad shoulders.

He held my gaze as his tongue licked between my legs, laving from anus to clit, one long wet trail, over and over, then once again. "*Christ!*" His head turned into my inner thigh, resting there, black eyes burning and wild as he panted, "Your scent…your taste." He nipped at my skin before returning to my drenched center, spearing his tongue deep.

My hips jerked and with his name on my lips, I watched him eat me, his eyes — intense, unwavering — on my face the entire time. The sight of his dark head between my sprawled thighs, his long tongue disappearing inside me, sliding in and out amid squishy sounds, rumbling growls, wet slurping, the pleasure evident on his face, was insanely arousing. He knew it would be. "Watch," he'd said.

He tongued my clit using long slow passes, back and forth, round and round, gradually building to quick lashes, sharp moist nudges, and everything inside me tightened, tightened, tightened…then exploded. With a cry, I bucked against his mouth, my hips jumping in his hands and a rolling sound of pleasure, masculine, wet and joyful, vibrated against my clitoris. I fell back against the pillow.

Before I caught my breath, Armand flipped my limp body over amid endearments whispered in two languages, and positioned me on all fours. His large hands slowly caressed my back, spanned my waist, skimmed along the flare of my hips to massage and squeeze my ass. From behind, one hand stole between my thighs and slid back and forth in the slippery cream along my lips. Mid-shudder, I spread my legs farther apart.

"*Bon, bebe, bon.*"

His voice equally as seductive as his hands, it stroked me in a warm caress, so enthralling my eyelids fluttered closed.

Armand's cock joined his hand between my legs. Under his guidance, its flared head caressed my wet folds in a lazy teasing pattern, slipping inside occasionally—just barely—before returning to circle my opening. It was maddening.

I groaned his name, rocked back against him, rotating my hips in entreating, circular passes. The bed squeaked a soft protest and a satisfied chuckle reached me seconds before the bed swayed.

Armand plunged his cock.

My shriek of "God!" mingled with his throaty groan of "*Dieu!*"

I shuddered and my fingers dug into the sheeted mattress. Embedded deep, his cock filled me, stretched me, thrilled me. Armand lay upon me, his skin smooth and hot, his body a heavy welcome weight, and began to pump, thrusting within me in languid sweeps. My inner muscles gripped him in a tight squeeze, drew him in as he thrust with long smooth glides, cock sliding in and out, and pace unhurried, he reached around to fill his hands with my breasts.

"You are incredible," he whispered hot against my nape. "Wondrous…and mine." He spoke in French between open-mouthed kisses pressed soft against my shoulders and back. I didn't understand what he said, but the way he spoke, low and sexy and intimate, set me on fire.

The afternoon sun fell on us, warming me further, and beneath our hands and knees, the bed squeaked a soft rhythmic song.

Armand rolled my stiff nipples between his fingers, thrusting his cock deep within me, whispering foreign words amid wet hot kisses, his leg hairs brushing crisp along the back of my thighs, and through me flashed overwhelming desire.

I pumped my hips in time with him, rotating with each thrust, legs spread wide, eager, excited, and Armand groaned before capturing the soft skin of my nape between his teeth.

His rhythm sped, thrusts turning wild and fast and urgent. One hand smoothed a caressing trail over my ribs, belly and pubic curls to finger my clit. Rubbing its slippery hood back and forth in quick short strokes, pounding into me from behind, my flesh caught firm between his teeth, Armand threw me into another rocketing orgasm. I bit my lip, jerking against him in a molten climax. A short cycle of drives followed, his pelvis grinding with each plunge, and with a groan, he filled me with seed.

My shaky limbs collapsed and I fell to the mattress, Armand a heavy blanket, while within me his cock still bucked and spurt. My spasms began to recede, slowing to soft mellow ripples, as he released my nape to press soothing kisses along my marked skin.

Fingers smoothed my hair aside, curling the wild strands behind my ear, and lingered to stroke my cheek. "Tell me," he purred his demand. "Tell me you're mine. Say the words."

God, yes! I thought. Absolutely. Every single inch of me. Every tiny atom. Yes-yes-yes! With a smile I said, "Maybe."

Against my nape, Armand's warm lips curved.

* * * * *

Sunday afternoon around 4:00, I answered the front door dressed in old shorts, a sleeveless white polo and a jaunty scarf tied around my throat. Jaunty? Okay, it wasn't, not by a long shot, but it did the trick and sufficiently covered my "love bite." Half-percent milk and a peanut butter and jelly sandwich on Wonder bread swam comfortably inside my tummy.

The door opened wide to reveal the mayor of Detroit City and his lovely wife decked out in all their finery—suits, tie, shiny new shoes. Holy shit. They beamed and I managed a sick smile in return. It was the best I could do—Jif was stuck between my teeth.

I hatched a quick plan to get the thank you's and the you're welcome's over and done with right out on the porch, but Aunt P spied them. She cooed and ushered the happy couple in before you could say Bridge Night Gossip.

At my door to express their gratitude? Give simple thanks to the stranger who saved the day, but more importantly, a designer leather handbag? Nah. They would have left the cameraman and reporter home if that were the case. They graced my door to get one thing and one thing only—their next sound bite.

Aunt P, the hostess with the mostess, served tea and crumpets (I kid you not) and looked pleased as punch to entertain the celebrated pair. It was a privilege. I endured an hour of it just for her.

Near the end of our little soiree, the mayor presented me with a plaque for bravery and good citizenship. My name's engraved on it, too. Neato and golly gee.

Aunt P and I walked them to the door and as the cameraman stepped over the threshold, a semi-white...thing darted inside the house.

"Oh," he said. "I let in your cat."

"I don't have a cat." I looked at the purring monstrosity wrapped around my legs. Once white, I'm sure, it appeared to have rolled in something. Something unpleasant. And smelly. It reeked of garbage, grime and garden dirt, not necessarily in that order. My nose wrinkled and I frowned at the thing before sneezing. Twice. A crooked tail swished to and fro, kinked in two spots, and its right ear was half-missing; the remaining stub barbed ragged and frayed.

After the door closed, Aunt P clapped her hands amid a peal of delighted laughter and gushed, "How exciting, sweetie pie—it's your familiar!"

Epilogue

My problems were few one short week ago…before *he* came to town. Now I have a new title to add to my resume: High Wiccan Priestess. And my powers, well, I've barely plumbed their surface. Who knows how vast and varied they are? Why, I could start levitating in aisle five of the corner grocery store next week or sneeze at work tomorrow and blow up something. It's a concern. Yep. The real challenge will be dealing with these bizarre newfound "talents" while keeping them secret from my best friend.

Speaking of whom, Nick called this evening with news that he tailed the second Whitcomb brother, Charles, to a friend's pool party today, where Nick caught him on tape in a tight red Speedo performing high flips and cannonballs off the diving board. Seems his back injury cleared itself up mighty quick. Must be a fast healer. Nick thinks we'll have Cambridge Services Group locked as a new client. Hopefully so, as we're submitting the case results to them tomorrow.

The feline intruder? Well, I refuse to acknowledge it as my familiar. No way. No how. Absolutely not. I even went so far as to shoo it back outside, but found it no less than an hour later in the kitchen scarfing Starkist off the good china. A smiling Aunt P looked on, smitten with the mangy ragamuffin. "I made appointments for first thing tomorrow with the vet and groomer, sweetie pie. Your familiar deserves nothing but the very best."

Yeah right, the very best. What am I, chopped liver? Don't I deserve a familiar that's clean? With two good ears? A straight tail? And you should see the circle of scarlet bites ringing my ankles, itching like there's no tomorrow. The wretched thing has fleas.

Early evening I met Chen for coffee at the local Starbucks. My invitation. I told him what I've known this entire week: I can't make a commitment—I've met someone else. The conversation hurt. Chen's a great guy, just not the great guy for me, and so to speed his recovery, I described my belief in witchcraft and magic and things that go bump in the night. He turned a little green. The date ended with the 'I hope we'll remain friends' speech. I meant it.

And the Frenchman? The one I'm absolutely crazy about but would rather be locked in a room packed with crazed chipmunks than admit it? That Frenchman? He dragged Aunt P and me into quite a dangerous pickle, that man did. Lied to me, too. He also saved his sister, covens both here and in France, and afforded me a way to avenge my parents' deaths. I guess I'll forgive him…eventually. But he owes me big time and I mean to collect! I'm talking wined and dined on actual dates. Courtship. Romance. The Whole Nine Yards.

After all, I've fought and won my first magical battle (all right, so I cheated and used a gun). The point is, I defeated my foe, I think I can handle one lone Frenchman. First on the agenda? Tonight's dream. Armand will find himself alone; I won't be there. Caffeine's my answer. I made a fresh pot of coffee.

I'm on my fifth cup.

Enjoy this excerpt from
SOMETHING WANTON
© Copyright Jacqueline Meadows 2004

Magic. Sorcery. Witchcraft. Believe in any of those? Nah, neither did I. Not until three months ago, that is, when I smacked face first into a few hard, irrefutable truths. Truths that turned my entire world upside down—bombshell discoveries—not the least of which concerned the revelation about myself.

You see—cue the suspenseful background music—I am a witch.

Yep it's true, cross my heart. And not just an ordinary witch, either (if such a thing exists); I'm told I'm a Wiccan Queen, a High Priestess. Nice title, huh? I'd kinda thought that's all it was, too, a silly moniker, just words. Oh, I knew my powers were stronger than average but I hadn't quite realized how much stronger. And the title? Well, it comes with baggage, the heavy Samsonite kind. I found out all about it the hard way, this past doozie of a week.

What happened? Glad you asked.

I'm a PI, and in addition to a normal workweek sleuthing cases of theft and adultery, I also fought two mystical battles, morphed a man into a toad, stopped a basement sexcapade gone awry, and rescued a tottering tree trimmer. I saved lives and took others. Did the week stop there? Give me a chance to catch my breath? No and no. It piled more atop me like a house of cards (and you know what happens eventually with those).

My week felt just as messy.

An example? Well, Thursday I came upon my 75-year-old aunt in a compromising position with the neighboring widower. *Very* compromising. Picture saggy birthday suits, tangled limbs, and septuagenarian sighs. My aunt raised me, she's essentially my mother, and everyone knows moms don't have sex. Ew. I'm still recovering from the sight.

But the real kicker? I discovered my best friend since childhood—one Nicholas Sage, and may I add the very married Nicholas Sage—has *feelings* for me, feelings that can't be filed under P for Platonic.

And oh yeah, I fell in love, madly, head-over-heels, crazy in love. Fell hard, too. I scraped my knees a bit but I'm fine now, better than fine, though I admit the fall was more 'hard tumble' than 'smooth descent'. See, for three months I fought a full commitment to him, fought harder still the loss of my heart.

But he fought back stronger, and he fought dirty.

About the author:

Jacqueline Meadows, wife and mother, lives in Michigan's thumb area where she feeds her addiction to steamy romance-- the hotter the better--with large daily doses of reading and writing.

Jacqueline welcomes mail from readers. You can write to her c/o Ellora's Cave Publishing at 1337 Commerce Drive, Suite 13, Stow OH 44224.

Why an electronic book?

We live in the Information Age—an exciting time in the history of human civilization in which technology rules supreme and continues to progress in leaps and bounds every minute of every hour of every day. For a multitude of reasons, more and more avid literary fans are opting to purchase e-books instead of paperbacks. The question to those not yet initiated to the world of electronic reading is simply: *why?*

1. *Price.* An electronic title at Ellora's Cave Publishing runs anywhere from 40-75% less than the cover price of the <u>exact same title</u> in paperback format. Why? Cold mathematics. It is less expensive to publish an e-book than it is to publish a paperback, so the savings are passed along to the consumer.

2. *Space.* Running out of room to house your paperback books? That is one worry you will never have with electronic novels. For a low one-time cost, you can purchase a handheld computer designed specifically for e-reading purposes. Many e-readers are larger than the average handheld, giving you plenty of screen room. Better yet, hundreds of titles can be stored within your new library—a single microchip. (Please note that Ellora's Cave does not endorse any specific brands. You can check our website at www.ellorascave.com for customer

recommendations we make available to new consumers.)

3. *Mobility*. Because your new library now consists of only a microchip, your entire cache of books can be taken with you wherever you go.

4. *Personal preferences are accounted for*. Are the words you are currently reading too small? Too large? Too...**ANNOYING**? Paperback books cannot be modified according to personal preferences, but e-books can.

5. *Innovation*. The way you read a book is not the only advancement the Information Age has gifted the literary community with. There is also the factor of what you can read. Ellora's Cave Publishing will be introducing a new line of interactive titles that are available in e-book format only.

6. *Instant gratification*. Is it the middle of the night and all the bookstores are closed? Are you tired of waiting days—sometimes weeks—for online and offline bookstores to ship the novels you bought? Ellora's Cave Publishing sells instantaneous downloads 24 hours a day, 7 days a week, 365 days a year. Our e-book delivery system is 100% automated, meaning your order is filled as soon as you pay for it.

Those are a few of the top reasons why electronic novels are displacing paperbacks for many an avid reader. As always, Ellora's Cave Publishing welcomes your questions and comments. We invite you to email us at service@ellorascave.com or write to us directly at: 1337 Commerce Drive, Suite 13, Stow OH 44224.

Discover for yourself why readers can't get enough of the multiple award-winning publisher Ellora's Cave. Whether you prefer e-books or paperbacks, be sure to visit EC on the web at www.ellorascave.com for an erotic reading experience that will leave you breathless.

Printed in the United States
25486LVS00005B/1-69

9 781843 609063